SMOOTH OPERATOR

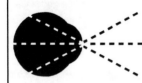

This Large Print Book carries the
Seal of Approval of N.A.V.H.

A TEDDY FAY NOVEL
FEATURING STONE BARRINGTON

SMOOTH OPERATOR

STUART WOODS
AND PARNELL HALL

LARGE PRINT PRESS
A part of Gale, Cengage Learning

GALE
CENGAGE Learning

Farmington Hills, Mich • San Francisco • New York • Waterville, Maine
Meriden, Conn • Mason, Ohio • Chicago

GALE
CENGAGE Learning

LIBRARY OF CONGRESS CATALOGING-IN-PUBLICATION DATA

Names: Woods, Stuart, author. | Hall, Parnell, author.
Title: Smooth operator / by Stuart Woods and Parnell Hall.
Description: Large print edition. | Waterville, Maine : Thorndike Press, 2016. |
   Series: Thorndike Press large print basic
Identifiers: LCCN 2016024641 | ISBN 9781410491473 (hardcover) | ISBN 1410491471 (hardcover)
Subjects: LCSH: Barrington, Stone (Fictitious character)—Fiction. | Intelligence officers—United States—Fiction. | Private investigators—Fiction. | Large type books. | GSAFD: Mystery fiction. | Suspense fiction.
Classification: LCC PS3573.O642 S63 2016b | DDC 813/.54—dc23
LC record available at https://lccn.loc.gov/2016024641

ISBN 13: 978-1-59413-985-7 (pbk.)
ISBN 10: 1-59413-985-7 (pbk.)

Published in 2017 by arrangement with G.P. Putnam's Sons, an imprint ofPenguinPublishingGroup,adivisionofPenguinRandomHouseLLC

Printed in Mexico
1 2 3 4 5 6 7 21 20 19 18 17

SMOOTH OPERATOR

1

Stone Barrington, clad only in a bathing suit and sunglasses, lay on the deck of the *Mary Lou* sipping a cool glass of Knob Creek. Stone was able to do that because Mary Lou Weston herself was manning the helm. Though perhaps manning was the wrong word. A striking blonde, she looked as if she'd be more at home on a runway than driving a boat.

"You sure you don't need me to do anything?" Stone called.

"On this little boat?" Mary Lou said. "I think I can handle it alone."

Stone smiled. Mary Lou referred to her *little boat* the way the genteel wealthy called their East Hampton mansions *cottages.* Granted, it was smaller than the *Queen Mary.* Still, it was one of the larger yachts on the Hudson River. Stone could practically walk across it to New Jersey.

"I was thinking more along the lines of

rubbing lotion on your back."

"My back?"

"I could work around to your front. I'm quite flexible."

"*MARY LOU,* PREPARE TO BE BOARDED!"

Startled, Stone rolled over and looked for the disturbance.

A Coast Guard cutter was bearing down on them.

"Hey!" Mary Lou said. "Those idiots are going to swamp us!" She flailed her arms, trying to wave off the boat.

The cutter kept coming. As it drew closer, Stone recognized the man with the bullhorn standing in the bow.

"Dino?" he said incredulously.

"You know that jackass?" Mary Lou said.

"So do you," Stone told her.

"No, I don't."

"Yes, you do."

"You're a hard man to find," Dino Bacchetti called.

Dino Bacchetti and Stone Barrington had been partners on the detective squad at the 19th Precinct. When Stone left the police force and passed the bar exam, Dino had stayed on. Over the years he had risen through the ranks, and not so long ago had been named police commissioner.

Mary Lou was steamed. "Who the hell do you think you are, stopping me in a Coast Guard cutter? You ought to be arrested."

Stone grinned. "I'm sure he should. Though you'll probably have a hard time finding a cop willing to do it. Mary Lou, allow me to present Police Commissioner Dino Bacchetti."

"Yeah, right," Mary Lou scoffed. "Like this joker's really the . . . Oh, my God!"

"Pleased to meet you," Dino called.

Mary Lou pushed the long blond hair off her face, and gawked. "What the hell is going on here?"

"I have no idea," Stone said. "Are you coming aboard?"

Dino grinned. "Nah. I just always wanted to say that. *Prepare to be boarded.* Actually, you're the one coming aboard."

"Gee, Dino, you're a nice guy and all that, but you don't have her looks."

"Sorry, Stone. It's not an invitation."

"You're putting me under arrest?"

"If I have to. I was hoping you'd come quietly."

"What's the charge?"

"Not answering your cell phone."

Stone spread his arms. "Do you see a cell phone?"

"Where are your clothes?"

"Below deck."

"Get them. You're going places."

"Where?"

Dino shrugged. "Frankly, I don't know."

2

"So, what's going on?" Stone said as the Coast Guard cutter skimmed across the water.

"Where's your cell phone?"

"In my pants."

"Get it out of your pants."

Stone dug in the bag of clothes he was carrying, pulled his cell phone out of his pants pocket. "Now what?"

"You have to call Ann Keaton. She's been trying to reach you all day. When you didn't answer, she got frustrated and called me."

"What does she want?"

"Damned if I know. She just wants you, and now isn't soon enough. I tried to stall her and she read me the riot act, implied that if I didn't locate you, the President would want to know why."

"She's trying to get me for the President?"

"She didn't say that. She didn't mention Kate except as a threat."

"I guess I better call her." Stone punched in the number on speed dial. "Ann, what the hell is going on?"

"Finally!" Ann said. "Can't you leave your cell phone on?"

"It's on and I'm calling. What is it?"

"Kate wants you at the state dinner."

"What state dinner?"

"The one tonight, honoring the French president."

"Tonight? Do you know what time it is?"

"Yes, I know what time it is," Ann said impatiently. "I've been trying to reach you all afternoon."

"The President wants me at a state dinner?"

"Yes."

"Why?"

"I don't know."

"What do you mean, you don't know? You're the chief of staff."

"That's right. I'm the chief of staff, and I don't know. I know *everything,* and I don't know this."

"All right, what *do* you know?"

"Dino will drop you at the heliport. You're taking a helicopter to Washington. A car will meet you there and take you to the White House."

"I don't get to land on the lawn?"

"That's just in the movies."

"No, they actually do it."

"Well, you don't. You land at the heliport. A limo will be waiting."

"I can't go to a state dinner. I'm wearing a bathing suit."

"No problem. Your car will stop at Henry Cassini's to pick up your new tux. They've had your measurements for two hours, they swear they'll be ready."

"You know my measurements?"

"I know which pant leg you put on first."

"I thought that was a state secret."

"It is. We'll have to disappear the tailor after he makes the tux."

"Seriously, what's this all about?"

"I wish I knew. I don't like things I don't know."

"Me neither. Will I see you this evening?"

"I'm afraid not. I have to go out to dinner with the congressman Kate bumped to make room for you at the table. Listen, I have to go. Will you apologize to Dino for me? I may have said some things that could be considered disrespectful to the office of the commissioner."

"Don't worry," Stone assured her, "I'll handle it." He clicked off the phone.

"So," Dino said, "what did she want?"

13

"She wants to know who you slept with to get the job."

3

Ann Keaton hung up the phone with a huge weight off her mind. Ann was an excellent White House chief of staff under normal circumstances, and she prided herself on handling crisis situations. Run in a last-minute guest for a fully booked state dinner? No problem. She had changed the guest list, arranged for a place at the table, even taken care of getting the new place card printed. And, when it turned out it would take some time to reach the surprise guest who didn't even know he was coming, she had arranged to have a tuxedo made, just in case when she finally located him he would not have access to his.

And then Stone Barrington had thrown a monkey wrench into her carefully laid plans by being totally unreachable.

Well, she'd handled the situation, and it had only taken a limousine, a helicopter, a Coast Guard cutter, and an intervention by the New York City commissioner of police. All in all, a pretty good day's work.

Now, was there anything else?

Oh, yes.

Ann sighed and picked up the phone.

Paul Wagner knew it was Ann. Her calls were important, and he'd assigned her her own special ring tone. He whipped his cell phone out of his pocket and slipped into his loving-boyfriend mode. Ann couldn't see his face, but it was important to get just the right vocal intonation.

"Hi, sweetheart," he said.

"Paul. Listen —"

Paul laughed. "Oh, for goodness' sake. I've had dinner reservations for two weeks. Do you know how hard it was to get them?"

"Something came up."

"It always does." Paul said it good-naturedly, but with just enough barb in it to keep her talking. "What's up?"

"It's silly, but I have to go out with a congressman."

"You're kidding."

"It's a spur-of-the-moment thing. He got bumped from his table to make room for a late addition of Kate's."

"You'll pardon me, but just who is so all-fired important he's interfering with our

16

dinner?"

"Stone Barrington."

Paul put just the right jealous-boyfriend inflection into his voice. "The man you used to be involved with?"

"He's not coming to see me, he's coming to see Kate. I have to take care of Congressman Jenkins, from East Podunk."

"Sweetheart —"

"I'm sorry. I'll make it up to you. I'm just in a bind."

Paul kept her on the phone as long as he dared, picking up as many details as possible, most of them silly and inconsequential, like tracking Stone down on the Hudson River and having to get a tux made at the last minute. Paul needed all the information he could get. It had seemed like a cushy job, cozying up to the attractive White House chief of staff, and he was happy to do it, but they weren't going to keep paying him unless he had something to show for it.

Paul had no idea whether this particular tidbit was worth anything, but evaluating the intel wasn't his job. His job was passing things along.

Paul punched the number into his cell phone.

4

Abdul-Hakim sized up the young man seated across the kitchen table from him. Salih was young and inexperienced, but his inexperience was what made him valuable. He was not on any watch lists, nor was he likely to be. An American citizen, the son of upstanding convenience store owners, he had no blot on his record.

"Are you ready?" Abdul-Hakim said.

"Yes," Salih said.

Abdul-Hakim was sure he was. It was Abdul-Hakim's job to know, just as it was his job to know every aspect of the operation. A handsome, clean-cut, Middle Eastern man in an Armani suit, Abdul-Hakim could have passed for a corporate CEO. In fact, he could have passed for many things, and did.

"One more thing," Abdul-Hakim said.

"What's that?"

Abdul-Hakim placed a box of rifle shells

on the table. "Use these."

"Why?"

Abdul-Hakim's smile was frosty. "Because I am asking you to. Use them, and leave the expended shell casing behind."

He reached in his jacket pocket, took out an ID, and slid it across the table. "This is also for you. A driver's license, in the name of Nehan Othman. This is what you will present at security, so they will not have a record of your name."

"I understand."

Abdul-Hakim slid a fat envelope across the table. "Ten thousand now, ten thousand more when it is done. I will not see you again until it is over." He stood up.

Salih stood also. "I will walk you out."

"No, you will not. You will wait here at least ten minutes before you even stick your head out the door."

Salih sat back down.

Abdul-Hakim's cell phone rang as he came out the front door of the apartment house. He pulled it out of his pocket and looked at the caller ID. It was the money man, the man paying him to set up and run the whole complicated operation. What could he possibly want now?

Abdul-Hakim tried to keep the irritation

out of his voice. "I just spoke to him. We're all set."

"Something came up."

5

Stone was ushered off the helicopter into a black limo driven by a liveried youth who looked barely tall enough to reach the gas pedal. He took off without a word and without even glancing at his passenger, drove skillfully into downtown D.C. and pulled up in front of the exclusive tailor shop of Henry Cassini. A sign on the door said CLOSED, but the lights were on inside. This was not unusual. Cassini lived above the shop and often worked late.

Before Stone could even ring the bell the door was yanked open by the tailor himself. An older man with sculptured white hair who was always impeccably dressed in finer suits of his own design, Cassini had a reputation for being genial and deferential to his customers. Tonight, however, he seemed slightly hassled.

"Come in, come in. I just finished." He cast an appraising eye over Stone and nodded. "They got the measurements right. Good. It's in the changing room. Put it on and come out."

The tux fit perfectly, as did the shoes supplied with it. Stone adjusted the bow tie and stepped out into the shop.

Cassini was pacing anxiously. "Let me see, let me see. Ah. Yes. Perfect. Turn around. Good. They got it right. You're all set. Take your wallet and keys, anything else you need. Your clothes will be sent on to your hotel."

Cassini ushered Stone back out the front door, where the driver was waiting by the car. Stone hopped in, and once more the driver took off without a word, and headed for the White House.

Stone settled back in the seat and watched as the lights flashed by in the gathering darkness. It was late for a White House dinner. He'd have missed the reception and would be lucky to get a cocktail before sitting down.

Stone felt himself tensing up. And it wasn't just the thought of keeping the President waiting. Kate Lee was a friend, wouldn't think him rude in any case, even if she hadn't summoned him peremptorily at the last minute. No, something else was wrong.

The car took a right-hand turn, and Stone realized what it was. The car behind followed them into the turn. It had been following them for some time.

"Take a left at the light," Stone said.

The driver was startled just to be spoken to. He half turned in his seat. "That isn't the way."

"Don't turn around. Just keep driving. Do what I say. I know you have your orders. I'm countermanding them. If you don't want to listen to me, tomorrow you can spend your last day on the job hearing a lot of people tell you why you should have."

"What's going on?"

"We're being followed. Don't turn around! Don't do anything out of the ordinary. Take a left at the light if you want to make sure. Watch the rearview mirror. When the lights come with us, you'll know I'm right."

The driver turned left at the light.

The car followed.

"Oh, my God!"

"Take it easy. Don't speed up or slow down. Don't react at all. Get back on course."

The driver made two rights and a left, coming out on the street they'd been on before.

The other car came with them.

"Who are they?"

"I don't know. Let's assume they're friendly until they prove differently."

"Like how?"

"Like that," Stone said, ducking low in his seat.

The block was dark. The window on the passenger's side of the other car slid down, and a long barrel emerged. The barrel flashed. A burst of gunfire shattered the rear window of the limo.

"Stay low!" Stone warned. "Do you have a gun?"

The driver was horrified. "No."

"Neither do I. All right, I have to get out."

"Now?"

"Yes, or they'll run us off the road and kill us both. Are there any curves in this road?"

"What?"

Another burst of gunfire made them duck. Stone gritted his teeth.

"I need a curve in the road to hop out. Are we near anything like that?"

"We're coming up on a traffic circle."

"Perfect. Step on it."

The young man hit the gas.

The circle had several streets running off of it. Nearly three-quarters of the way around was a dark alley.

"Keep right through the circle. Slow down

as you hit the other side, then go like hell. Whatever happens, just keep going. As soon as I'm out of the car, drive straight back to the dispatcher and turn it in."

"Out of the car?"

"Don't think, just drive. Slow down now."

The driver slowed the car.

Gunfire raked the side window. The car in pursuit was overtaking them. The alley was just ahead.

"Go!" Stone yelled.

The driver hit the gas.

Stone wrenched open the door and flung himself from the car in a sideways roll, arms folded over his chest, chin tucked in. He landed on his side, rolled over several times. He came out of the roll slightly dizzy, stumbled to his feet, and staggered down the alley.

As he had hoped, it had all happened too quickly. The tail car had followed the limo past the mouth of the alley. It would have to back up, or go around the circle, or try to find him on a side street, any one of which would give him the time he needed.

Stone ran down the alley. His left leg hurt, but nothing seemed broken. He came out of the alley into the street and tried to flag down an oncoming cab. The driver went on by. So did the next cab. The third cab

25

stopped.

Stone hopped in. "Take me to the White House."

The driver turned around and stared. "Are you sure?"

"Yes. And hurry."

The driver shrugged and took off.

Stone leaned forward, checked his appearance in the rearview mirror. His hair was mussed, his face was smeared with dirt, and the right-hand sleeve of the tux jacket had separated at the shoulder. Inches of white shirt could be seen between the jagged edges of the seam.

Stone leaned forward to the driver. "Scratch that. Take me to Henry Cassini's."

"They're not open this late."

"I know. Take me anyway."

"You're the boss."

The driver pulled up in front of the tailor shop. Stone hopped out and leaned on the bell.

A few minutes later a very indignant Henry Cassini pushed aside the curtain in the door. The look on his face changed when he saw who was ringing.

The little tailor pulled the door open. "What is it?"

"There's a problem with the tux."

6

A White House aide led Stone past the head table, where President Kate Lee and First Husband and ex-President Will Lee were entertaining the French president and a host of VIPs including the Senate Majority Leader and the Speaker of the House.

Dinner was in full swing. The guests were already enjoying the first course of caviar and quail eggs.

The aide made sure Kate noticed Stone's arrival, then led him across the dining room to his table.

Stone was clearly sitting with the lesser lights, not that he minded. The empty seat at the table was next to a stunning redhead in a low-cut blue ball gown.

Stone pulled out his chair and sat down. Waiters rushed to bring him his appetizer.

The redhead arched an eyebrow and said, "Nice of you to join us."

"I almost didn't make it at all. I had a

wardrobe malfunction."

She smiled. "I could have helped you with that. I'm very good with clothing."

Stone smiled. "I don't believe I've had the pleasure."

"You certainly haven't," she said, holding out her hand. "Margo Sappington. White House legal counsel."

"Really?" Stone grinned, shaking her proffered hand. "I'd have thought for that position you had to be stuffy and senile."

Margo smiled and leaned against him playfully. "Just what position did you have in mind?"

A white-haired man across the table pointed at Stone in a preemptive manner. "Excuse me. I don't believe I caught your name."

"Stone Barrington."

"I've heard of you. I don't recall your connection to politics."

"I'm a lawyer," Stone said, as if that explained it all. "And you are?"

"Congressman Marvin Drexel, North Dakota. You realize you're very late."

"It was unavoidable."

"A congressional logjam is unavoidable," Drexel said pedantically. "Lateness is merely bad judgment."

"A congressional logjam is only unavoidable when obstructionist morons put party ahead of country."

"God save me from men who parrot talking points!" Drexel snorted. "You weren't supposed to be here, were you?"

Stone smiled and pointed. "I think that's my name tag."

"It was my understanding Congressman Jenkins would be at this table."

"Really? Are you wrong often?"

An elderly man at the table burst out laughing. "Got you there, Marvin." He reached out to shake Stone's hand. "Sam Snyder, congressman, Maryland. Democrat, I might add. Which is why Congressman Drexel has been ignoring me."

Stone laughed politely, but merely smiled and nodded, hoping to forestall the conversation. Sam Snyder had a kindly, avuncular nature, and struck Stone as the type of man who'd latch on to you at a wedding and bore you to distraction with benevolent goodwill. The last thing in the world Stone wanted was to get involved in a political squabble between two rival congressmen.

Luckily, Margo came to his rescue. She plucked Stone by the arm and said, "So you're a lawyer, too. Maybe that's why they put us together."

"I'm not sure that's the reason," Stone

said, "but whoever arranged the seating, I'd like to thank him."

"Are you here alone?"

"Yes."

"Me too. So much nicer to pair up with someone than be the third wheel to some married couple."

"I'll drink to that."

The rest of the dinner progressed smoothly. Caviar and quail eggs gave way to a summer salad from the White House garden, followed by an entrée of dry-aged rib-eye beef.

Margo was in heaven. "This steak is to die for!"

Stone smiled. "It's good, but I've had better."

"Oh? Where?"

"Elaine's."

"Elaine's?"

"In New York City. On the Upper East Side. She died, and the restaurant closed. A shame. Elaine was wonderful. I always ate there."

"Didn't Woody Allen used to hang out there?"

"No, *I* used to hang out there. But I let Woody drop in from time to time."

Margo laughed, and dug into her rib eye.

By the end of dinner Margo was flirting

with Stone in a way the congressmen doubt-less found distracting. At one point she practically leaned into his lap. She came up giggling and holding a cell phone. "This was on the floor. Yours?"

"Yes, thanks." Stone slipped it into his pocket.

Margo's eyes twinkled. "Did you do that on purpose?"

"What?"

"Put it there so I'd lean over?"

Stone laughed.

Congressman Drexel watched their banter with growing irritation.

Dinner was followed by a command per-formance of a violin concerto featuring a French virtuoso. "Where'd they find one?" Stone whispered.

Margo put her hand over her mouth to keep from giggling.

Finally the last note ended. Before Stone could suggest they retire elsewhere, an aide tapped him on the shoulder. "I understand you need to make a phone call."

Stone shook his head. "That wasn't me."

"Yes, it was. If you would follow me, please."

"He has a cell phone," Margo said.

The aide shook his head. "It's from an-other phone."

Stone shrugged helplessly. "If you'll excuse me, it seems I have to make a phone call."

Margo slipped a card into his hand. "Just in case you have to make another."

Stone followed the aide across the banquet floor and out the double doors. Instead of taking him back the way he had come, the aide ushered him through a service door marked NO ADMITTANCE.

Stone found himself in a narrow back corridor. Halfway down the hall was a desk with a phone, but they sailed right by it, followed a labyrinth of back passageways, and emerged in a small antechamber. The aide gestured for Stone to sit down.

There was a phone on the desk next to him. "Is this where I'm supposed to make a call?"

"No. When the intercom buzzes, don't answer, just get up and go in."

The young man went back out the way they'd come, closing the door behind him.

The intercom buzzed a few minutes later. Feeling like a fool, Stone got up and pushed his way through the door.

He entered the Oval Office and found Kate Lee sitting at the coffee table with the Speaker of the House.

"Ah, good, you're here. Come in, sit down. You know Congressman Charles

Blaine?"

"Only by reputation, we've never met."

The congressman did not rise to offer his hand, but he looked up and his face told the story. This was a man on the brink of despair.

"My God, what's wrong?" Stone said.

Kate took a breath. "What I'm about to say doesn't leave this room."

Stone figured he was being warned largely for the congressman's benefit. Kate knew he'd be discreet.

"Of course."

"As you may be aware, the congressman and I had a meeting this afternoon."

"I think everyone is," Stone said.

The meeting had been widely reported, and rumors were rampant. The fact that the Republican Speaker of the House was having private meetings with the Democratic president was significant, particularly in light of the current congressional session. Several crucial votes were coming up, and the prospect of a bipartisan compromise had led to wild speculation. The political news shows could hardly talk of anything else.

"Congressman Blaine and I are supposed to be ironing out our differences. To a certain extent that is true, but it's not the reason for this meeting."

"Then what is?"

Congressman Blaine looked at him with pleading eyes. "My daughter's been kidnapped."

7

Stone stared at the congressman. "What?" he said incredulously.

"I got a call Sunday night on my cell phone," the Speaker said. It was as if a dam had broken, and the words all poured out. "I almost didn't answer, because it said Unknown Caller, but I did. It was a man. I'd never heard his voice before, but he had a slight accent. He said he had my daughter, and if I ever wanted to see her alive again I'd listen carefully and do exactly what he said."

"Which was?"

"Stay away from the police. If I contact the police or any authorities whatsoever, she's dead. I know that's what kidnappers always say, but he meant it. He said it was a deal-breaker. The police, the FBI, the CIA, the Secret Service, anyone. If I told anyone, they'd know, and they'd kill her and disappear."

"How much do they want?"

"They don't want money."

"What do they want?"

"Votes," Kate said. "They want his votes. They wanted him to get in touch with me, to propose a bipartisan initiative. Or what was *supposedly* a bipartisan initiative. His job was to line up enough votes to pass a bill the Republicans were blocking in the House."

"They said if I didn't do it, they'd kill my daughter. If they didn't see immediate evidence of me reaching out to the President, they'd kill my daughter. That's why we're having these meetings, and that's why they're publicized."

Stone turned to Kate. "How long have you known?"

"Only since this afternoon. A few days ago Charles came to me with his bipartisan proposal. I was stunned, but of course pleasantly surprised by the outreach. Then he arranged the meeting this afternoon, insisting it be given media coverage. Only when he got here —"

"I broke down. Told her everything. I couldn't take it anymore. I've been carrying this around with me all week. I hadn't told anyone."

"Why today?"

Blaine sighed. "This came this morning." He reached into a manila envelope, pulled out a paper, and passed it over.

It was a rap sheet. The mug shot showed a blond college-aged girl. The charge was felony possession of a controlled substance. Her attorney had gotten it down to a misdemeanor, and she had paid the fine.

"They're threatening to expose this?" Stone said.

Blaine shook his head. "It's public knowledge. I campaigned on it. If it could happen to my daughter, it could happen to yours."

"Then what's the point?"

"I don't know. That's what scares me. They have my daughter and they sent me this. What can it mean?"

"I have no idea," Stone said. "So what are you going to do?"

"Anything they want."

"Specifically."

"There's a bill coming up in the House regarding medical benefits for wounded vets."

"They want you to block it?"

"They want me to pass it."

"What's the problem?"

"It's a clean bill. The Republicans want to vote it down in favor of an amended bill guaranteeing no portion of the medical benefits would go to birth control. They're demanding that the clean bill sails through, or they'll kill my daughter."

"So what if it does?"

"I'll be a Judas, the betrayer of my party. But I don't care if it would save her."

"Can you swing the votes?"

"Probably. There's one hard-line conservative who might block me."

"How?"

"Debate it to death, kill the bill. If he doesn't get his way, he'll filibuster until my daughter's dead."

"Who is that?"

"Congressman Marvin Drexel."

"He was at your table, Stone," Kate said. "Did you get a read on him?"

"Oh, yes. Congressmen Blaine's assessment seems accurate."

Blaine raised his eyes to Stone. "What do I do?"

"Have they offered proof of life?"

"No."

"Next time they contact you, demand proof of life. Tell them if you get it, you'll swing the vote."

"Demand? I can't make demands."

"You can and you must. They're not going to kill her just because you ask. If they do, they lose their leverage. Just let them know you're ready to give them what they want. They'll be eager to make that happen."

"If you think so."

"Let's be brutally honest. Either your daughter is alive or she's dead. If she's dead, nothing you do can change that. If she's alive, we want to keep her that way. We have to sell the idea that her kidnappers get nothing if they don't."

"What do I say?"

"Say you're too upset to continue if you don't know she's alive. Don't rehearse it too much. Just start talking and it'll all come pouring out."

"Go home and do as Stone advises," Kate said. "We'll take it from here."

As soon as the congressman left, Stone turned to Kate. "How much of that is true?"

She looked surprised. "You think he made it up?"

"Not for a minute. I mean what you told him, that you haven't contacted anyone but me."

"That's the truth. If I do something and his daughter dies, I'd never forgive myself."

"That's what I figured. Who knows about this?"

"No one, not even Will."

"That doesn't add up."

"Why not?"

"Someone took a shot at me on my way here."

"What!"

"I was followed when I left the tailor shop. They fired shots, and tried to force my limo off the road. That's why I was late. Expect an extra charge for the tux."

"So what can you do?"

"What do you expect me to do? You want me to find his daughter, but no one can know I'm looking for her. But someone obviously does. The question is how. What about the aide who brought me in here? What does he know?"

"Just to tell you you had a phone call and leave you in the antechamber."

"That's all?"

"That's all."

"And who gave him those instructions? Clearly you didn't."

"Ann did, and she didn't blab to anyone. She wasn't even here."

"You didn't talk to anyone at the CIA? Holly Barker, for instance. Maybe not about the kidnapping, but to mention I'd be in town?"

"Are you accusing me of being indiscreet?"

"No, Madam President, just human. The

point is, someone knows I'm here, and they'll be keeping tabs on me. I can ditch a shadow, but not long enough to investigate. I may have to get outside help."

"You'd bring in Dino?"

"In a heartbeat, if I could think of a cover story. But I have someone better in mind."

"Who?"

"That's on a need-to-know basis. At this point, I think you need some plausible deniability."

8

The woman slid into the driver's seat of the Porsche 911 GT3 RS, started the engine, and switched on the lights.

A man rose up in the shadows of the backseat and held a straight razor to her throat. "Hello, Pamela," he said.

"Cut," cried Peter Barrington. "Good for camera? Good for sound? Print it, new setup, let's come in for the close-up from the killer's POV."

Peter pulled his cell phone out of his pocket. It had vibrated during the take, and now it read **Missed Call**. He hit the callback button and stepped away from the street set where he was filming on the back lot of Centurion Studios.

"Hi, Dad. What's up?"

"You got time to talk?"

"A little. We're in between takes."

"How's the picture coming?"

"Couldn't be better. The cast is great, and

the dailies look fantastic. We're getting plenty of coverage, and the editor has more footage than she needs. I wish they were all this easy."

"Is your new producer working out?"

"Just fine. Not that I don't miss Ben, but Billy's a natural. We're actually ahead of schedule."

Dino's son, Ben, had been producing Peter's films ever since they graduated from Yale drama school, but recently he'd been elevated to the head of Centurion Studios, leaving Peter without a producer.

"Is Ben around?"

"He drops in now and then. He's the head of the studio, he can make his own schedule."

"So he could help you out if you needed anything?"

"I suppose so. What's going on?"

"Do you think you could get along without Billy for a few days? I've got a sticky situation and could really use his help."

"It's important?"

"You wouldn't believe."

"Then take him."

"Are you sure?"

"Don't worry about it. I'll be okay."

"Great. I'll give him a call."

"Hang on, Dad. He's on the set, I'll get

him for you."

Billy Barnett was overseeing the camera move, which was going smoothly. Billy had a way of making things happen without seeming to push, a valuable asset for a movie producer. Union men couldn't be hurried, and didn't take kindly to the suggestion they might be dogging it. But Billy had an easy rapport with the crew, and he was a big reason the film was coming in ahead of schedule.

Peter tapped Billy on the shoulder and crooked a finger.

Billy followed him away from the set. "What's up? We got a problem?"

Peter shook his head, held up his cell phone. "You have a call."

"Oh, really?" Billy took the phone. "Hello?"

"Hello, Billy," Stone Barrington said. "Do you know who this is?"

"Yes."

"What are you up to?"

"Shooting night scenes for Peter's movie."

"How's it going?"

"Great. I'm really getting into this whole producer thing."

"Glad to hear it. Think you could come to Washington, D.C., for a while?"

"Are you kidding?"

44

"No."

"I'd rather be shot dead."

"I understand. But I'm afraid it's a matter of national importance."

"Come on. You're in Washington. Don't they have that agency — what do they call it? — the CIA?"

"Sorry, I can't use the CIA. I need you."

"Aw, hell," Billy said. "I'd have to check with Peter."

"I did. It's fine with him."

"Then I guess I've got to go."

"How quick can you get here?"

"It's too late to catch the red-eye. I can get a flight tomorrow morning."

"That won't do. I need you here tomorrow morning. Can you fly Peter's jet?"

"Sure, if he lets me borrow it."

"Tell him I said so. You can't fly commercial anyway, if you're going to bring your stuff."

"I gather I should come prepared for . . . certain eventualities?"

"Be prepared for anything."

"Where are you staying?"

"Don't come by the hotel. Can you make an eleven o'clock brunch?"

"What restaurant?"

Stone chose one within walking distance of his hotel.

"Okay. See you there."

Billy gave the phone back to Peter and managed to herd him away from the set.

"Your dad wants me to borrow the Cessna."

"Really?"

"Yeah. Is that a problem?"

"I have a lesson, but I'm sure Tim can scare something up."

Tim Peters was the pilot who managed the hangar and handled Peter Barrington's flying lessons.

"If it doesn't work, call your dad. This is his party."

"No big deal. I'll get along fine."

"What do you mean by that?"

"You still have to give Betsy the news."

When Billy first met his wife she'd been working at a Las Vegas casino under the name of Charmaine. She'd changed her name to Betsy when they ran off to L.A., and they'd been married under the names of William and Elizabeth Barnett. Billy had gotten her a job as Peter's assistant. She'd proven invaluable, and had been working for him ever since.

Billy found her conferring with the script supervisor.

Betsy saw him coming and smiled. "Hi, honey. I was just taking a look at those two lines you mentioned. It makes sense to cut them, but Peter will have to sign off on it."

"I'm pretty sure he will," Billy said. "They can always fix it in the mix, but if they shoot it they'll have an awkward jump-cut to deal with. It's so much easier just to leave it out."

"Don't worry. I'm on it."

"Good." Billy took a breath. "Honey?" he said hesitantly.

Betsy knew that tone of voice. She sighed. "Oh, hell."

9

Stone checked into the Hay-Adams Hotel and discovered Ann had booked his favorite suite. In addition to the usual amenities, three shopping bags were displayed in the sitting room.

One held his bathing suit and the clothes he'd left at the tailor's, and another held several sports shirts, slacks, underwear, socks, and casual shoes.

The third held an electric razor and various assorted toiletries.

Stone put the toiletries in the bathroom and hung the pants and shirts in the closet, where he also found a sports jacket.

Ann had done her job well.

There was a knock on the door. Stone opened it, expecting to find the bellboy with some forgotten amenity.

Margo Sappington stood in the doorway. "I hope you didn't think you were going to get away from me that easily," she said.

"I really wasn't trying."

"Going to invite a girl in? Or should I stand here in the hallway?"

Stone stepped aside. Margo came in and glanced around the room.

"Nice spread. You got a girl tucked in the bedroom?"

"Not yet."

"Oh, big talker. Suppose you're not my type?"

"Then I'd have to wonder what you're doing here. Would you like a drink from the minibar?"

"An outrageously priced ounce of whiskey? Who could resist?" Margo kicked her shoes off and sat on the couch.

"On the rocks?" Stone said.

"Not if you have to go looking for them."

Stone checked the bar. Ann had gone the extra yard in making sure it was stocked with Knob Creek. He poured Margo a glass, then one for himself, and sat on the couch next to her.

Margo tossed hers off in one gulp. She set down the glass. "I think we've spent enough time with social graces. It's been a long evening." She leaned into Stone, pressed her body against his. "I believe in getting to the point." She smiled. "In fact, I think I feel it now." She reached her hand down to his crotch. "Oh, yes. What a lovely greeting."

Margo stood up and stepped out of her gown. Stone rose to kiss her, cupping her breasts while she unbuttoned his shirt and unzipped his pants.

Naked, they fell onto the bed. Stone slipped his hand between her legs. She was already wet with anticipation. She climbed on top, reached down, thrust him inside her. He rose to meet her. She raised her head and arched her back, resembling nothing so much as a spectacular figurehead on a boat. It was all Stone could do to hold back and let her finish at the same time he did.

Afterward she lay across his chest, traced her finger around his nipple.

"If it's not too much to ask," she said, "where did you go in such a hurry?"

"It's not too much to ask. It's too much to answer."

"You weren't trying to get away from me, were you?"

"Heaven forbid."

"Because I'm hard to shake."

"Don't tell me you're a stalker."

"Nothing like that. I saw you, and I had to have you."

"I enjoyed myself. If you enjoyed yourself, we might get another chance."

"Might?"

"Let me amend that," Stone said. "I think the chance is arising now."

The chance not only arose, it involved a variety of positions.

10

Billy Barnett walked off the Centurion Studios back lot and hopped into the 1958 D Model Porsche Speedster parked in the space reserved for the producer. Billy was five-ten, 175 pounds, with short-cropped brown hair, graying at the temples, a wiry, athletic-looking man of about fifty-five.

Except when he wasn't.

Billy Barnett, aka Teddy Fay, could be anywhere from five-eight, 160 pounds to six-two, 220, his age anywhere from forty-five to eighty-five. With the right makeup he could be an elderly Jew, a young Hispanic, or a middle-aged Muslim.

In his twenty years at the CIA, outfitting agents for assignments, Teddy had learned the game well. He could disguise himself as anyone, create the identity, upload it into the CIA database, the FBI database, as well as those of the NSA and Homeland Security. He could create documents from passports to driver's licenses, from credit cards to agency IDs.

He could also delete from the mainframe any identities no longer useful. Before leaving the CIA Teddy had carefully erased all his own fingerprints and photographs. For all intents and purposes, Teddy Fay had ceased to exist.

Teddy drove out to the Santa Monica Airport and pulled up in front of Peter Barrington's hangar. Teddy had found the hangar for Peter, paved the way for him and his father to buy it on the cheap from a rock star who was selling off his aircraft and looking to dump the storage space. It was a nice setup, big enough for one jet and two smaller planes. At the moment it held Peter's Cessna Citation Mustang and Teddy's turboprop.

Teddy got out of his car, left the motor running and the lights on, unlocked the office, and fumbled on the wall for the switch.

A gun barrel jabbed him in the back of the neck.

Teddy couldn't believe it. After a lifetime of diligence, the most clever, careful, and resourceful agent in the history of the agency, who had eluded an international manhunt orchestrated by the upper echelon of the CIA, was about to be brought down like this.

And he had only himself to blame. He had grown complacent in his new life as Billy Barnett, with his wife and his house and his job and his normal daily routine. That and the fact that no one was looking for him anymore.

Teddy had been on the run ever since leaving the agency. He'd had to be. The charges against him, including murder, were so numerous it was hard to imagine a conviction that would not result in a life sentence. Teddy had resigned himself to being a fugitive all his life.

He probably would have been if he hadn't helped Peter Barrington by dealing with some Russian mobsters who were stalking him. Teddy, disguised as Billy Barnett, had followed Peter to L.A., where he secured a job at Centurion Studios outfitting movie actors with weapons and rigging explosions.

Then he teamed up with Peter's father to stop a terrorist attempt to detonate a nuclear weapon in L.A. Stone revealed Teddy's role in the matter to then-president Will Lee, and obtained a presidential pardon, ending the CIA manhunt. Teddy had been able to settle down, though prudently not under his own name.

And, irony of ironies, his routine lifestyle

had made him lazy and careless, and now he was about to die.

"Put your hands on your head."

Teddy let out a breath and thanked his lucky stars. He'd been spared. This was no seasoned hit man. This was a rank amateur who didn't know what he was dealing with.

Teddy complied immediately, raising his hands to the back of his head.

Then he spun like a flash, lunging sideways and chopping down.

The gun rattled to the concrete floor. Teddy ignored it. He grabbed the man's arm, twisting it around and down.

The man came to his feet, his face contorted in pain. He flailed at Teddy ineffectively with his left arm while Teddy twisted his right. Teddy dropped to the floor and scooped up the gun. It had a silencer. That was what had poked him in the neck.

Teddy scowled at his assailant. Even in the dark he looked young and inexperienced. Teddy snorted in disgust. "I'm sorry, kid, but you're just no good at this. Who hired you?"

The young man said nothing and set his jaw.

"I don't have time for you to be coy. If you don't want to talk, I'll shoot you. Who hired you?"

"No one hired me."

"You do this just for fun?"

The young man's eyes flashed with determined resignation. "For the cause!" he said, and lunged for the gun.

Teddy shot him in the head.

11

Teddy switched on the light and examined the corpse. He was a young man, even younger than Teddy had thought. A blond all-American boy, perhaps a college student. The shot was a through-and-through, entering his forehead and exiting behind his left ear. Teddy fished an old newspaper out of a garbage can and slipped it under the kid's head to catch the pooling blood. He found the bullet on the hangar floor, slipped it into his pocket.

Teddy checked his watch. It was ten o'clock, one in the morning in D.C. He was cutting it close. The small jet would have to refuel twice going cross-country. It was doable, he just hadn't figured on having to dispose of a dead hit man.

Teddy scampered up the stairs. There was a small apartment that came with the hangar. He and his wife had lived there for a while, and only moved into a house when they thought the coast was clear. When they had, Teddy had left much of his old life behind.

He went in the bedroom, grabbed a suitcase, and tossed in a handful of clean clothes, some useful caps and jackets, mostly reversible, and some sports clothes.

In the room that had served as his office, he spun the combination for the large safe he'd installed. He took out his sniper rifle, the one he'd handcrafted for himself at the CIA, and the small .380 semiautomatic pistol with a silencer he'd built to fit into the barrel.

He took out a lockbox, selected a passport, driver's license, and credit cards in the name of Frank Grisham, and another set in the name of James Byrd. From the ID photos, Grisham was older and practically bald, while Byrd was young enough to sport brown hair with a thick mustache. He added several other identities, including credentials of all types in various names with various ID photos.

Teddy took out his makeup kit, along with the hairpieces, putty, glue, facial hair, and prosthetics he would require for these identities.

Teddy locked the safe, took everything downstairs, and loaded it into Peter's Citation Mustang.

Teddy searched the body. According to his driver's license, the man Teddy had killed was a twenty-two-year-old kid named Alan Johnson. According to his student ID, he was a sophomore at UCLA. According to his car registration, his parents had money. The kid drove a brand-new Lexus.

Teddy checked the exit wound at the back of the head. The blood had almost dried. He found an old canvas and rolled the body in it. He opened the bay doors, drove his Porsche into the hangar, and closed them again. He popped the trunk, wedged the kid inside. It took a little doing.

There were few cars in the parking lot at that time of night, and Teddy had no problem finding the young man's Lexus. Luckily, there was no streetlight nearby, and the car was backed into a head-in space. Teddy backed in next to him, popped both trunks, and transferred the body and the silenced gun. He hopped in the Lexus, started the engine, and headed out of the lot.

He ditched the car in a dark alley about a mile from the airport. The distance was probably overkill, but Teddy wasn't taking any chances. He was rusty, or the kid never would have got the drop on him. Teddy liked his new life and didn't want to lose it.

He couldn't afford to be careless. He took pains wiping down the car, then hoofed it back to the airport.

On his way he whipped out his cell phone to call Peter on the set. He was in luck. They were in between takes, and Peter picked up.

"Hey, Peter, I know you're doing me a lot of favors, but I need one more. You got room to put Betsy up while I'm gone?"

"How come?"

"I'm hoping it's an unnecessary precaution. But if I didn't take it, I'd never forgive myself."

"You think she's in danger?"

"I think someone might try to get to me through her."

"You got it."

"Don't alarm her, but don't take no for an answer."

"Relax. I'll handle it."

Teddy hung up the phone with a huge weight off his chest. He hurried back to the airport, drove his car into the hangar, and cleaned up any trace of the intruder.

He filed a flight plan he had no intention of following, and took off for Washington, D.C.

12

Salih showered, shaved, and put on a suit and tie. He picked up his attaché case and checked his appearance in a full-length mirror. Perfect. He felt a little anxious, but that was only natural. He'd be fine.

Salih took the Metro downtown and joined the crush of commuters heading for work. He walked down the block and went into an office building.

At the front desk, the security guard asked him where he was going, and he named a company on one of the higher floors. The guard nodded, asked him for a photo ID. Salih fumbled in his wallet for the driver's license Abdul-Hakim had given him. The guard took it and compared Salih's face to the photo. When they matched, the guard said, "Nineteenth floor," and handed the ID back. He didn't even write down Salih's name.

Salih took the elevator up to the nineteenth floor. Two people got off with him. One went into the office near the elevator. The other went into the office he'd named.

Salih waited until they were gone, then pushed his way through the fire door to the service stairs. He went up two flights, stepped over the chain, and went up the steps to the roof.

The door was unlocked, as he'd been told it would be. He pushed it open and stepped out onto the roof.

It took a moment to get his bearings. To his right was the back of the building, so the street was on the left. He crept to the edge of the street side and peered over. It was a long way down, but Salih had no fear of heights. He watched the traffic in the street below, slow-moving during rush hour. It would thin out soon.

Salih had a good view of the entrance across the street. People were arriving for work. He was early.

Salih set his attaché case on the roof. He knelt down, clicked it open, and raised the top.

His sniper's rifle fit as perfectly as if the case had been made for it, which indeed it had. Custom built to look like an attaché, the case boasted a snug but carefully pad-ded space for every piece of the disassembled sniper's rifle, from the stock to the scope. There was even a space for the box of shells Abdul-Hakim had given him. Not that he would need them. One bullet would be sufficient, even at such a distance. He had spent enough time on the range to be sure of that. Nonetheless, Salih had packed the whole box of bullets. It was better to take them than risk having to explain why he hadn't.

Salih took out the scope and lined up the entrance across the street. It was crystal clear in the scope. He might as well have been standing right there.

Now for the hard part.

Waiting.

Salih found a nice spot where he could sit with his back against a chimney. He set his case on the roof, and carefully assembled his rifle.

13

At eleven o'clock sharp, Teddy Fay, disguised in his James Byrd identity, stood in the street outside a restaurant reading the *Washington Post* and observing Stone Barrington through the front window. Stone sat alone at a table in the back, nursing a cup of coffee.

None of the diners appeared to be paying any attention to Stone, and no one seemed to be watching from the street. Teddy might have felt reassured, except someone had tried to kill him last night, and he had no idea what the hell was going on.

Teddy whipped a burner phone out of his pocket.

Mike Freeman, CEO of Strategic Services, the prestigious private security firm, scooped up the phone in his New York office. "Freeman."

"You know who this is?" Teddy said.

"No."

"You once tried to hire me."

"Ah, yes. You ready to take the job?"

"Not just yet. I need a favor."

"I'm more inclined to do favors for agents who work for me."

"I don't think you'll mind. It's for the benefit of a mutual friend."

"Who might that be?"

"The guy who introduced us."

"What do you want?"

"Got any agents in D.C.?"

"What do you think?"

"Good. Here's what I need."

"Mr. Barrington?"

Stone Barrington looked up from the table. "Yes?"

The young man placed a cell phone on the table. "Mike Freeman wanted you to have this."

"Why?"

"He wants you to make a call from this phone." The agent rattled off a phone number.

"You don't have it written down?"

"I was told not to."

"Say it again."

The agent did. Stone committed it to memory. "Anything else?"

"No, sir."

"You can go."

As soon as the agent left, Stone punched in the number.

Teddy Fay answered on the first ring. "You know who this is?"

"Yes. Why the cloak-and-dagger?"

"Your phone's been hacked."

"How do you know?"

"I'll explain later. We have to assume our meeting's blown. Pay your bill, go out the front door, turn right, walk two blocks, and turn left. Keep your cell phone on. When you reach the other side of the street, raise it to your ear. Don't look to see who's following you, that's my job. Start now. Leave your phone on, pay your check, and go."

Stone couldn't help glancing around for assassins as he paid his bill. He went out, followed Teddy's directions. As he crossed the street he raised his phone to his ear to receive further instructions.

"Go down in the Metro, buy a fare card but don't use it, stick it in your pocket, go right back up the same stairs."

"Are you serious?"

"I'm not just serious, I'm cautious."

Stone went down in the Metro. He put five bucks in the machine and bought a fare card. He stuck it in his pocket, went back up the stairs, and raised the phone to his ear.

"You did good," Teddy said.

"What do you mean?"

"Buying the Metro card. Nine people out of ten would have made a show of pretending they'd changed their mind about taking the train. You just bought the card and left."

"Doesn't mean I didn't feel like a fool. Was anyone following me?"

"Yes, me. See the greasy spoon on the corner?"

"I do."

"Let's go in there."

"Why?"

"Is it one you ever use?"

"Hell, no."

"Then I like it."

Stone walked into the diner. It had a Formica counter with metal bar stools, and a row of booths.

"Sit at a booth."

"They're all taken."

"Sit at the one I'm at."

Stone looked again. Teddy Fay, in the persona of James Byrd, sat at the booth in the corner. It took Stone a moment to reconcile the younger man with the brown mustache with the man he'd last seen as Billy Barnett.

Stone slid into the booth. Teddy signaled for the waitress. "I'll have coffee now, more when the order comes. Give me scrambled eggs with bacon and sausage."

"I'll have coffee and an English muffin," Stone said.

The waitress left, scribbling the order.

"Already eaten?" Teddy said.

"Hours ago."

"Figures. What's up?"

"This conversation never took place."

"That's my favorite kind."

"I need your help."

"I'm an associate producer. Are you making a movie?"

"No."

"Too bad. I'd like to make a movie."

"You have the particular talents necessary for this job. You've been erased. Obliterated. A complete and total data dump. I can Google you and come up empty. I can run your fingerprints and not get a match. You don't exist, which is exactly what this job needs. Plausible deniability."

"You're making it sound irresistible."

"Wait until you hear the pay scale."

"What's that?"

"Absolutely nothing. Technically you don't get expenses. In reality I'll pay for lunch."

"Do I get a thank-you?"

"Actually, no. That would mean acknowledging you'd done something. Trust me, no one wants to do that."

"Heaven forbid."

"If it goes well, you get to watch on television while everyone else takes the credit." Stone cocked his head. "Sound good to you?"

"Hey, you had me at 'this conversation never took place.' So what if it doesn't go well?"

"That would not be good."

"Will I be alive?"

"That would be the desired outcome."

The waitress came back, slid coffee in front of them. Teddy dumped in cream and sugar, stirred it, and took a big gulp.

"Look, Stone. Your son's a stand-up guy. I like working for him, I like coming up with neat ways to kill people and no one gets upset, they put it in the script. I like having a wife and a home and a job. I owe you for the presidential pardon. Without it, I'd still be on the run. But it's retroactive, and *only* retroactive. It's a pardon for everything I've *done*. But it's not a license to kill. I kill someone else, I'm back on the run."

"I understand."

"No, you don't."

"What do you mean?"

"I already did."

"What?"

"That's the reason for the fun and games. Someone tried to kill me when I went to pick up Peter's plane. And who knew I was going to do that? Absolutely no one, unless they were listening on your phone."

"Who tried to kill you?"

"A college student, of all people. It makes no sense."

"No kidding. Someone took a shot at me, too."

"When?"

"Last night, when I was on my way to the White House."

"The White House?"

"That's right. There's a lot you don't know."

"Which is not a good position for someone people are trying to kill. What the hell is going on?"

"Yesterday afternoon the President summoned me to the White House to attend a state dinner. It was a last-minute invitation. I was rushed here by helicopter, fitted into a tux that had been sewed for me that afternoon. Between the tailor shop and the White House, someone took a shot at my car."

"Who?"

"I didn't stick around to find out. I jumped out of the car, tore my tux, went back to have it stitched, got to the dinner late, and sat at a table with an attractive young lady lawyer and a bunch of stuffy old congressmen. After dinner I was smuggled into the Oval Office, where the President was meeting with the Speaker of the House."

"I know about that."

"No, you don't. The bipartisan initiative is a ruse. Someone kidnapped his daughter and is going to kill her unless he can swing enough Republican votes to pass the Democratic version of the veterans aid bill."

"And Kate knew about this all along?"

"No, she found out yesterday afternoon. Up till then she thought the Speaker was making bipartisan overtures. When she found out what was going on, she called me in."

"Why?"

Stone looked at him.

"No offense meant," Teddy said, "but she's the President of the United States and used to be head of the CIA. Surely she doesn't have to rely on an ex-cop from New York."

"That was the whole point. The Speaker

71

was told not to involve the authorities or they'd kill the girl. She thought she could bring me in under the radar."

"And you figured the same thing about me."

"Well, there's nobody more under the radar than you. Your presidential pardon cleared your record. For all intents and purposes, you do not exist. Who better to find the congressman's daughter than the man who isn't there? Plus, you actually have skills. If you could outwit the CIA for years, you ought to be able to deal with some kidnapper."

"Thanks for your support. That sounds good in theory. In point of fact, it means zero. I can't find the girl without looking for her, so the kidnapper will know *someone* is. He won't know who, but that doesn't matter. The fact it's happening is what puts her in danger."

"I understand that."

"So, basically you're asking me to get the girl killed so you don't have to."

"I'm counting on you to be smart enough not to."

"Okay, so far you're the weak link. You get brought on the job, someone tries to kill you. You bring me in, someone tries to kill me. The only way they know I'm involved is if someone hacked your phone. Can I see it?"

Stone took it out, handed it over.

Teddy pried the back panel off. He reached in with the tine of a fork, popped out a little clip. "There you go. That's the source of your trouble. Who had access to your phone between the time you were summoned to Washington and the time you called me?"

"No one."

"Then where did the bug come from? I'd rethink that position."

The waitress slid their orders onto the table. The eggs were greasy, but Teddy took no notice. He dug in as if taking on fuel. Stone could see his mind churning.

"You sleep with her?"

"Who?"

"The pretty lawyer who sat next to you at dinner."

"She showed up at my hotel room."

"No kidding. That's how your phone got bugged."

Stone shook his head. "I called you before that."

"Yes, but *after* dinner."

"Oh, hell."

"What?"

"She picked my cell phone up off the floor."

"During dinner?"

"Yeah."

"Bingo." Teddy buttered some toast. "Okay, the lady lawyer's one possibility. The question is how did she know you'd be at the dinner? How'd you get summoned to the White House?"

"You wouldn't believe it."

"Try me."

"Dino Bacchetti tracked me down on a young lady's yacht on the Hudson River to tell me to call the President's chief of staff."

"How the hell'd he do that?"

"In a Coast Guard cutter."

"Who's the chief of staff?"

"Ann Keaton."

"Didn't you used to be involved with her?"

"That was a while ago."

"What happened?"

"When Kate won the presidency Ann became chief of staff. I'm in New York, she's in D.C. She has a lot of responsibilities."

"And another man?"

"She may have a boyfriend."

"Okay, she's a possible source. And there aren't many." Teddy waved the waitress over for more coffee. He watched her move off and said, "Tell me about the kidnapping."

"The girl's been gone since Sunday night. The Speaker got phone calls warning him not to go to the police, followed by an anonymous letter."

"A ransom demand?"

"No. It was a photocopy of his daughter's arrest record."

"She has one?"

"She got busted for pot in college. Her lawyer got it down to a misdemeanor and she paid the fine."

"And the Speaker would pay to hush it up?"

"You'd think so. He's a conservative antidrug crusader. But everybody knows about the arrest — he even campaigned on it. 'My own daughter got busted in college — if it can happen in my family, it can happen in yours. What if pot is just the beginning?' Pretty effective. Makes you overlook the way drug laws are putting poor people in jail while rich offenders go free."

"So why did they send it?"

"The congressman doesn't know. As you can imagine, he's hysterical."

"All to swing a vote?"

"Apparently."

"Who knows this?"

"The congressman, the President, me, and now you. That's it. Not even the ex-

President knows."

"She's holding out on her husband?"

"So she says. If they're whispering in the bedroom, there's no way to know."

Teddy mopped up his eggs with the toast. "And you want me to fix it."

"I know it's a lot to ask."

Teddy pushed back his plate. "I'm going to do it, and not just because I owe you. I know you don't want to ask me any more than I want to say yes. But you did and I will. I'll tell you why. If it wasn't for the fact that there is a congressman involved, this is a run-of-the-mill kidnapping. The most ordinary of crimes. But I'll do it for the same reason you had to ask."

Teddy took a big gulp of coffee.

"This isn't what it seems."

14

Congressman Marvin Drexel sat up straight in his desk chair and gripped the phone tighter than usual. "No, I *don't* know what's going on, and I don't like it. Blaine's up to something. He won't return my calls. We need to line up defenses, find some congressmen we can hold. I'm having lunch with Radner and Newbridge and I'm confident I can bring them on board. But after that, I'm scrabbling."

Drexel slammed down the phone, leaned back in his chair, and rubbed his chin. How did things get so fouled up? Last week everything was fine. Suddenly it's all falling apart. The Speaker was up to something, a most unexpected development given that the Speaker was a hard-line conservative as steadfast as they come. Just the idea that he was reaching out to the President would be enough to sway some of the least powerful congressmen, the ones who would fear losing their districts if a bill allocating money for wounded vets passed and they'd voted against it. And Congress would never get to vote on the amendment.

The worst thing was it was *his* amendment. He'd added it with much fanfare, tacked it onto the veterans aid bill, a rallying cry to his fellow Republicans, greeted with overwhelming support. If the clean bill were to be voted through, it would be a personal slap in the face, a disaster of epic proportions, the type of blunder that endangered reelection.

And now he was late for lunch.

The congressman slammed out the door, took the elevator down to the lobby. It was crowded around one PM when the whole world was going out to lunch. He usually beat the crowd, but today he got a late start.

He wondered if he should take a cab. It was only four blocks to the restaurant, but he was too keyed up to walk. It would take too long, and he needed to get there quickly, relax his mind. It wouldn't do to let people see he was shaken. He had a reputation for being precise, always poised, even under pressure. He couldn't afford to appear uncertain.

He came out the front door, looked to see if there was a cab. If there was, he'd hail it.

If not, he'd walk.

His head exploded as the bullet ripped through his brain.

15

On the rooftop across the street Salih methodically dismantled his rifle and packed it away in his attaché case. He snapped it shut and went through the stairway door that he had carefully left wedged open. He walked quickly down three flights, slipped through the fire door, and rang for the elevator.

In the lobby Salih found everyone hurrying toward the street. He blended into the crowd, and pushed to the front as if to get a better view of the action across the street.

Not that anyone could see anything. Three police cars had arrived, and sirens announced more were on their way. Officers had barricaded off the sidewalk and were preventing people from crossing the street.

Salih pushed his way through the crowd. At the corner he went down in the Metro. He rode three stops, came out of the subway, and walked down the street to an abandoned garage. He unlocked the padlock on the corrugated metal door and slid it upward.

The garage was dark. There were no lights, and either there were no windows or they had been painted out. After a minute his eyes became accustomed to the light and he saw a gray Chevy sedan, there as promised. He opened the door and the light went on. The key was in the ignition. He tossed his briefcase in the front seat.

"Were you followed?"

Abdul-Hakim was there. Salih hadn't heard him come in. He spun around to see the familiar thin, swarthy face, darker than usual in the shadows of the garage.

"No. I took precautions."

"You're wrong. I followed you."

"So what? You know me, and you knew I was coming. No one else followed me."

"True. But I had to be sure."

"Do you have the money?"

Abdul-Hakim pulled a fat envelope out of his pocket. "Ten thousand, as promised."

Salih tore the envelope open and riffled through the bills.

Abdul-Hakim shot him in the head. Salih had a second to register sheer amazement, before he fell to the garage floor.

Abdul-Hakim bent down and plucked the

envelope from Salih's hands. He rolled the dead man over, reached in the pocket of the gray suit jacket, and removed a similar envelope. He checked to see that it also held ten thousand dollars. He tossed the two envelopes onto the front seat of the car. He found Salih's wallet, removed the fake driver's license, and replaced the wallet. When he was done searching the body, he dragged Salih to his feet and hefted him over his shoulder.

On the far wall of the garage, a freezer unit purred quietly. Abdul-Hakim carried the dead sniper over, raised the lid, and flopped him in. The body fit fine.

Abdul-Hakim closed the lid and locked the freezer with a padlock. He got in the car and backed out of the garage. He stopped in the middle of the sidewalk, hopped out, pulled the garage door down and locked it. He hopped in the car, backed out into the street. As he drove off, he took out his cell phone and made a call.

16

Calvin Hancock watched the coverage of Congressman Drexel's assassination on the gigantic screen on the living room wall of his penthouse apartment. Calvin had several other abodes, including a villa in Rome, a chateau in Versailles, and a country manor in Gloucestershire, to name a few, but he tended to gravitate toward penthouses because they offered him the most privacy.

His penthouse in Washington was a floor-through duplex, with its own elevator. He had security at the ground floor, of course, but upstairs he was completely alone.

Calvin Hancock was a money man cast from the Koch brothers mold, a kingmaker of such power and importance that his endorsement could make or break a career. If Calvin Hancock backed you, you were in. In the last election Calvin Hancock had spent over a quarter of a billion dollars trying to keep Kate Lee from being elected.

The fact that he failed had been a bitter pill to swallow.

The phone rang.

Calvin Hancock checked caller ID and snatched it up. "Yes."

"It's done," Abdul-Hakim said.

"I know it's done. I'm watching television. Believe it or not, it made the news. What happened last night?"

"What do you mean?"

"Stone Barrington showed up at the White House dinner. Alive, needless to say."

"You called at the last minute. The best men were not available."

"Then you should have gone yourself."

"I was working on a backup plan."

"Is it taken care of?"

"It is. We're monitoring his phone calls. Will that be sufficient, or would you like me to arrange a second attempt?"

"That will do for now. What about the movie producer he called?"

"It's taken care of. We had him met at the airport."

"Here?"

"There. In Santa Monica."

"That's fast work."

"We had an ISIS recruit from UCLA, an impressionable fanatic. He was happy to get the job."

"Are you sure he's trustworthy?"

"It doesn't matter. He doesn't know anything."

"All right. Good."

That was the word Abdul-Hakim had been waiting to hear. Without Calvin Hancock's approval, a job was never done. Now he could move on.

"What next?" Abdul-Hakim said.

"The girl."

17

Karen Blaine lay on the bare cot and plotted her escape. They picked the wrong girl when they kidnapped her. Karen wasn't some helpless pushover, too frightened to be any problem. A straight-A student with an analytical mind, Karen was used to figuring things out. Her situation was just another problem to be solved.

She was in a small room with no windows and a wooden door. It was an old door, really old, the kind that locked with a skeleton key.

The room was unfurnished except for the cot. There was a metal sink deep enough to fill a mop bucket on one wall, and a toilet in what at first glance appeared to be a closet. At one time this had been a workroom. Now it was a jail.

Her captors were the odd couple. There was the Arab, the smarmy, well-dressed Middle Eastern man who'd kidnapped her from campus. He probably wasn't an Arab, but she dubbed him that, a useful shorthand. He spoke good English, with just a trace of an accent.

The big man was another story, a run-of-the-mill American goon, dressed like a slob in a tattered T-shirt so worn she couldn't make out the rock group depicted on the front. The big man was dumb as a board, not that he ever talked to her, besides grunting out commands. She'd given up trying to talk to him. He just ignored her, or at most muttered for her to shut up. It was clear he wasn't the brains of the operation, just the muscle.

Karen had no idea why she was here. She assumed it had something to do with her father. That was the danger of being the daughter of a prominent, powerful man. Her father had always warned her to be on her guard, but she'd never taken him seriously.

Clearly she'd been wrong, and now she was paying the price. She never should have gotten into the man's SUV, but he had CIA credentials. He'd looked like a CIA agent, and acted like one, too, with his suave, efficient manner, and he had such a plausible story: he'd been sent by her father, it was an emergency, and she had to come at once.

Her heart was pounding when she climbed into the front seat of the SUV. He'd leaned over to buckle her seat belt, and the next thing she knew she woke up here.

Wherever here was. It could have been right near campus or it could have been a million miles away. There was no way to tell with no window and not even the smallest crack to peek through. Karen never even knew if it was day or night, let alone what time it was. She measured out her days in sandwiches. She'd been here for eight or nine sandwiches; she wasn't sure when she'd started keeping track.

The big man was the one who brought the sandwiches and took away the empty plates. He never brought her anything useful, like a fork she could bend the tines of to make a key. The meals were sandwiches, for the most part processed cheese with mayonnaise on white bread. Nonetheless, every time she heard the key in the lock Karen glanced up expectantly, hoping this time he would bring her something she could use. But he never did.

What she needed, of course, was something to pick the lock. She had a simple coiled bedspring she'd found hanging from the frame of the cot, and she'd spent a lot of time trying to twist it into a key, but no matter what shape she bent it into the round wire wasn't substantial enough to move the tumblers. And there wasn't anything else in the room that might work.

There came the familiar sound of the key in the lock. The big man stuck his head in the door. He did that now and then, just to reassure himself she was there. He never came any closer. It was as if he didn't trust himself with her. Or as if he didn't trust her with him.

That didn't stop Karen from trying.

"It's you. Thank goodness. I need my purse. I know you have it. You took it from me. There's a book in it. I'm going nuts. I need to read. *Please* bring me my purse."

The big man gave no sign he even heard her. He just turned around and left.

Karen wasn't crushed. It had been a long shot, first that they even had the purse, second that they'd let her have it. There was nothing in it that she could use for a weapon except pencils and pens, and they'd be sure to take those. Still, they wouldn't let her have it.

There came the sound of the key in the lock. Karen's heart leaped. Was it possible?

The big man came in and her hopes were dashed. He had the paperback thriller she'd been reading.

He brought the fucking book!

"Oh, thank you, thank you," Karen said. "But I can't read it. I need my glasses. They're in my purse. Can you get me my purse, please?"

Without a word he set the book on the floor, went out, and slammed the door. Again she heard the key in the lock.

What were the odds this time? The ice had been broken. He'd given her one thing, he could give her another. Conversely, he'd made a goodwill gesture and she'd slapped him down, complained about it, said it wasn't good enough. He'd never do it again.

There came the sound of the key in the lock and the big man was back. He didn't have her purse. He had her glasses. He set them on the floor and went out.

Karen snatched them up.

The glasses were broken. The screw had come loose, and one of the plastic temples had fallen off. She never found the tiny screw. It probably would have been stripped anyway. But she'd managed to repair the glasses.

The temple was held on by a safety pin.

18

Lance Cabot, director of the CIA, scowled at the men assembled in his office. "I have to brief the President in half an hour, and I don't know what I'm going to say. Who wants to fill me in?"

The agents looked at each other. One of the field directors spoke up. "Sir, we flooded the area with agents, but there is no sign of the shooter. It's difficult. We're tripping all over the D.C. police."

"I'm not interested in excuses. What *is* being done?"

"The attack came from the roof of the building across the street. We pinpointed it rather quickly. The windows of the building do not open, but the roof gave the optimal angle. An expended cartridge shell was found there, and it's consistent with the type of sniper rifle that would have been used in the attack."

"And no one saw the sniper?"

"It's a busy office building. Before the attack no one would have noticed. After the attack everyone rushed for the street."

"I understand. What's being done?"

"We're questioning everyone. So are the police."

"And the overlap?"

"Anyone who saw anything is being shunted from us to the cops to Homeland Security to the FBI to the NSA. All those interviews are being compared and coordinated to see if they add up to anything.

"At the same time we're screening hundreds of hours of surveillance video from the cameras in the building, with an emphasis on the elevators and the upper floors."

"With what result?"

"It's early yet, but we have no reports of anyone carrying anything long enough to have contained a rifle. Several reports of men carrying briefcases which could have housed a disassembled rifle. No metal cases. Ruling out soft leather cases and messenger bags, we get standard-size hard cases, black, brown, and tan. Carried by men of all descriptions — white, black, Asian, and Middle Eastern."

"What are we tracking with regard to terrorist activity?"

Another agent spoke up. "Sir, we have

eleven high-ranking suspected terrorists in the D.C. area. None could be the shooter. All are under surveillance, and ironically, our own men give them alibis."

"Which proves nothing. They'd have ordered it done anyway."

The intercom buzzed.

Lance scooped up the phone. "I said hold my calls."

"You want this one."

"Is it the President?"

"No."

"Then I don't want it."

"Yes, you do."

"Margaret —"

"You hired me to screen your calls. Take this one, or fire me and hire someone whose judgment you trust."

Margaret hung up.

Lance scowled at the phone. Line two was blinking. He exhaled, pressed the button on the line, snarled, "Yes?"

The young man on the phone stammered. "S-sir."

"Who's this?"

"It's Jenson, at ballistics, sir. I'm running tests on the shell casing found on the rooftop across the street."

"Yesterday's news, Jenson. I'm being briefed on it now."

"I noticed something I thought you'd want to know."

"What's that?"

"The cartridge was standard CIA issue."

Lance blinked. "Run that by me again."

"It's an exact match for the rounds we issue. I can't imagine how an assassin would have gotten his hands on one."

Lance didn't say anything.

"Sir?"

"Who knows this?"

"Only me. I just noticed myself."

"Okay. Sit on it and I'll get back to you."

The others were looking at Lance expectantly. He made a show of slamming down the phone, and snorted impatiently. "Everyone thinks their business is so fucking important. All right. Anyone got anything new?"

No one did.

"Get out of here and get me something. Frankly, we got caught with our pants down."

As soon as they were gone Lance snatched up the phone. "Margaret?"

"Sir?"

"Did you tell anyone about this?"

"No, sir."

"As long as you don't, you can keep your job. Call the guy back, give him the same message. Tell him not to put it in his report."

Lance hung up the phone, leaned back in his chair, rubbed his forehead. A dull, persistent ache seemed to be settling in. One he hadn't felt in a while.

The situation had unpleasant connotations for Lance. He could think of only one other instance of a congressman killed by a sniper with a CIA background.

Could Teddy Fay be alive?

Lance logged onto the CIA mainframe, plugged in the name Teddy Fay.

Nothing came up.

Lance wasn't concerned. For years any mention of Teddy Fay had been classified information that would not show up on such a lowly level.

Lance entered his personal security codes, instituted years ago and changed every week primarily for the purpose of keeping Teddy Fay out.

Nothing.

Lance pushed himself back from the computer, breathing hard. The assassination of a congressman in his town, on his watch, was bad enough. But the thought that his nemesis might have come out of hibernation and begun another reign of terror was almost more than he could bear.

Lance pulled himself together and picked up the phone.

19

In her office in the West Wing of the White House, Holly Barker, newly appointed assistant to the president for national security affairs, and former CIA station chief, answered the phone. "Yes?"

"Holly, Lance. Ready for the briefing?"

"I'm ready to be briefed. I've got nothing to contribute."

"No one does. It's way too early. Unfortunately, that's not the type of remark the head of the CIA can make with impunity. CIA directors are supposed to know everything the instant it happens."

"It's a tough job anytime, Lance. I'm sure it's tougher now."

"Yeah. Listen. Something came up. For your eyes only, not to be bandied around."

"I'm not a gossip, Lance," Holly said tartly.

"I never said you were."

"What's up?"

"You know we found a shell casing on the roof of the building across the street?"

"That much I know."

"It's CIA issue."

"Oh?"

"Like the type we'd issue for a company sniper rifle."

"Are we admitting to issuing sniper rifles now?"

"Don't piss me off, Holly. You and I both know someone who spent twenty years issuing exactly that type of equipment to company agents."

"What are you trying to say?"

"Is it possible Teddy Fay's back?"

"Don't get paranoid on me, Lance."

"What is Teddy Fay's official status?"

"Teddy Fay doesn't exist."

"That's what bothers me. I just looked him up on the mainframe and came up empty. No history, no records."

"That's because he was pardoned. His record was wiped clean."

"Not from *us*! No one deletes *our* records."

"Clearly they do."

"I don't like it. This assassination has Teddy's MO all over it."

"Teddy has a new identity and a new life. A second chance. Do you really think he'd risk that just to screw with you?"

"I don't have all the facts."

"That's why you're grasping at straws. You're desperate for something to tell the President. Trust me, it's not Teddy Fay."

"How can you be sure?"

"It's impossible, Lance."

Holly hung up the phone.

Teddy Fay was sitting across the desk from her. He had changed from his James Byrd disguise into the more comfortable persona of Fred Walker. Fred was closer to his age, and had CIA credentials.

Holly hadn't initially recognized Teddy as agent Fred Walker. He'd had to tell her who he was. But this was not surprising, as Teddy's gifts with disguise were legendary. Teddy had actually taken Holly to the opera once, at the height of the FBI manhunt, and she'd never suspected the elderly opera enthusiast sitting with her was the object of her chase.

"That was Lance," Holly said.

"I gathered."

"He wanted to know if you shot the congressman."

"Not *that* congressman. Anything else?"

"A spent cartridge believed to come from the sniper's rifle was CIA issue."

"Interesting. And that reminds me. I could

use some ammunition."

"Teddy."

"Relax. I'm here to help."

"With the assassination?"

"The assassination is the tip of the iceberg."

"Lance is holding back?"

"Lance doesn't know."

"Doesn't know what, Teddy? What were you about to tell me when he called?"

"Kate hasn't told you?"

"Hasn't told me what?"

"Of course. You couldn't tell me if she had. We have a very delicate situation under way and everything is on a need-to-know basis. That includes you, and even the President."

"You didn't say that includes you."

"I need to know. At the moment Stone Barrington is the only one who knows everything. I'd bring him in here to vouch for me except he's being watched."

"Can I call him?"

"No. His phone was hacked. I destroyed the bug, but we can't be sure it's the only one. The President's in a bad situation. She asked for Stone's help. He came to me. Now I'm bringing you into the loop. The daughter of the Speaker of the House has been kidnapped. The kidnappers are forcing him

100

to meet with the President and arrange for the passing of the veterans aid bill."

"And Kate knows this?"

"She's the only one who does. Even Will doesn't know."

"What about Lance?"

"Lance doesn't know, either. He can't. If there's any sign of police or CIA involvement, they'll kill the girl. There's been a leak, but we don't know from where. If we alert the CIA, the kidnappers will know about it, and the girl is dead."

"And the assassination?"

"It's undoubtedly connected. Congressman Drexel was a conservative stumbling block in the way of passing the bill. Anyway, the President was desperate. She didn't know where to turn, so she brought in Stone. He told the Speaker to demand proof of life next time the kidnappers contact him. He told the President not to do anything, just appear to be moving forward with the bipartisan agenda and he'd take it from there. That's where I come in."

"I thought you were done with all this."

"I owe Stone for the presidential pardon. Plus I owe the President. And this thing is scary. When Stone called me, I was on a movie set in L.A. An hour later someone tried to kill me. I take that personally."

"So that's the situation. The President's holding out on you. Now you're holding out on her. You're also holding out on Lance and everyone else in the world, with the exception of Stone Barrington. Thank goodness you and he see eye to eye."

Holly and Stone had been an item once, ironically back in the days when they were hunting Teddy Fay.

"One thing I don't understand," Holly continued.

"What's that?"

"If I can't tell anybody about this, what do you expect me to do?"

"I'd like to log into the CIA mainframe. They keep installing safeguards to keep me out. I could get through them easy enough, with the right equipment, but I just don't have the time. Log on for me, will you?"

"That's all you want?"

"That would disappoint you? No, Holly, that's not all I want. You're CIA, but as the President's advisor, you're not responsible to Lance. He can't give you orders or make you tell him anything, not that he'd know what to ask. But you're privy to whatever information his investigation turns up. Stone and I need you to coordinate with us and try to figure out what's going on, because there's no way it could be as simple as it seems.

"We have to rescue the girl and take the pressure off the congressman. We're ill equipped to do it. The minute we start looking into her disappearance, the kidnappers will become suspicious and they'll kill the girl. Of course they'd lose their leverage, but I hate to tout that as the upside."

"So?"

"So we have to investigate the kidnapping without making any waves. I can't show up on a college campus and chat up the girls in the dorm without raising a bunch of red flags. I need a young female agent who can pose as a friend of the girl, who hasn't heard from her in a few days and is concerned. She's got to be smart, clever, intuitive, personable, and able to blend in. Do you have anyone like that?"

Holly smiled. "As a matter of fact, I do."

20

Teddy Fay took one look at the young woman who walked into Holly Barker's office in a sheath dress with high heels, studded earrings, hair fastened in a bun, and said, "She won't do."

Millie Martindale blinked. "I beg your pardon?"

"I need someone who can blend in on campus. She looks like she's going to a cocktail party."

"Do you have any casual clothes in your office?" Holly said.

"Yes."

"Go make yourself look like a college student."

The girl who came back five minutes later looked nothing like the one who'd just left. In a sweater and blue jeans with her hair down and her makeup off, Millie could have passed for a college coed.

"What do you think?" Holly asked.

"Not bad. I'd say the pencil behind the ear is pushing it, but she'll do." Teddy turned to Millie. "Are you CIA?"

"I'm Holly's personal assistant."

"That's not what I asked. Do you report to Lance Cabot?"

"No."

"Do you know Lance?"

"I've met him."

"Does he know you?"

"Yes."

"Then don't let him see you like that. Can I count on your discretion?"

"Absolutely," Holly said.

"I'm asking her."

"I'll do anything *she* tells me," Millie said.

"What if she tells you to listen to me?"

"I'll do it."

"You have any friends in the CIA?"

"I know a few agents."

"Are you close friends with any of them?"

"No."

"She has a friend in the FBI," Holly volunteered.

"Boyfriend?"

"They have a relationship."

"Who's the guy?"

"Quentin Phillips. He worked with us on a joint CIA-FBI operation recently. Good man."

"I'm sure he is." Teddy turned to Millie. "Can you freeze him out?"

"Sir?"

"This whole operation is on a need-to-know basis, and he doesn't need to know. In fact, it could be fatal. I'm not saying you can't see him, I'm saying you can't tell him. Can you do that?"

"Yes."

"All right," he said to Holly. "I'll take her on your say-so because time is tight." He turned to the girl. "What's your name?"

"Millie Martindale."

"I'm pleased to meet you, Millie," Teddy said. "I'm Fred Walker. But you didn't meet me. In fact, this conversation never took place."

"Is this about the assassination?"

"No. This is about the kidnapping of an undergraduate student from Georgetown University last Sunday. Without raising any alarms, mingle with her classmates, find out who saw her last, who she was with, and whether she had any intention of going somewhere."

"Why is she important?"

"She's the daughter of the Speaker of the House."

Teddy reached in his jacket pocket and took out a piece of paper. "Here's a printout about the girl. Read it and shred it. Google her and check her out on Facebook, that's where I got this. But don't do it on a White House machine. Go out to a library and rent computer time. Learn everything you can without printing anything out. No one knows she's been kidnapped, and we need to keep it that way."

"Got it."

Millie went out the door.

Holly looked at Teddy. "Satisfied?"

"She'll do. Now, if you wouldn't mind helping me out with this computer."

"You really need me to log on for you?"

"If you do, it won't look like unauthorized access."

"And it will if you do? You're slipping, Teddy."

"I'm rusty, and I haven't slept in thirty-six hours. Come on. Be a sport."

"What do you want from our database?"

"Any recent terrorist activity. Which group is rumored to be responsible for the assassination if no one is taking credit for it. Report of sleeper cells on college campuses."

"I can request all that."

"Not without people knowing you're looking."

"Of course I'm looking. There's been a

terrorist attack. Everyone is looking."

"I like to get my own perspective. First-hand information."

Holly gave him a look. "All right, don't tell me."

She began typing, entered her top security passwords, logged on, and got up.

Teddy took her place, rubbed his hands together, and clicked the mouse, entering the restricted CIA site.

Teddy surveyed the home page with satisfaction. His fingers poised on the keyboard, he smiled up at Holly Barker.

"Don't you have a meeting?"

21

Abdul-Hakim sat on the couch and planned his next move. It was hard creating an illusion of terrorism.

He was no extremist. Far from it. Had he not been kicked out of the Wharton School of business he might have been a junk bond trader by now. Abdul-Hakim resented it. Cheating on exams hardly seemed an expellable offense. For most business positions it was practically a prerequisite. No matter. He now stood to make more than any of his former classmates.

His team for this mission had been carefully comprised of a disparate group of Islamic fanatics and American thugs. This was not just of necessity — fanatics were hard to come by — but part of the plan, one of Calvin Hancock's requirements.

The whole grand terrorist plot was designed to unravel upon the slightest inspection. All it would take was a push in that direction, and that had been planned. Then all the discrepancies would begin popping up. The CIA bullet, for instance. Nothing in itself, but telling once taken in context.

Abdul-Hakim smiled, and went back to his plans.

It wasn't working. The safety pin from Karen's glasses was the right size for a key, but it just didn't work. If the pin was closed, it would fit in the lock but it wouldn't turn. If she unpinned the pin and straightened it out, the big end was just the right size to fit in the lock and move the tumblers, but she couldn't get a good enough grip on the pointed end to twist it.

If was horribly frustrating. The point of the pin was sticking into her finger, but she barely noticed. She was sure it would work, if only she could make it turn.

Abdul-Hakim's train of thought was broken by the girl's jailer, who came lumbering into the living room and stood, dumbly, staring at him, as if waiting for instructions.

"Yes?" Abdul-Hakim said.

"When we gonna move the girl?"

It was actually a good question. This house was a temporary situation only, a fine place to stash the girl for a few days, but it wouldn't suit their ultimate purpose. For that they'd need someplace isolated, and the transport would take time. The round-trip would take three hours he could have spent on something else. On the other hand, it would get the big goon out of his hair. From that point of view it was probably worth it.

Abdul-Hakim considered. All right, what did he have to do? Nothing that urgent. He shoved his briefcase aside, and set his black satchel on the coffee table.

He popped the satchel open and took out the hypodermic syringe.

Blood from the pinpricks in Karen's finger-tips was making the pin slippery and hard to hold. She licked the blood off, but the saliva was just as bad. Nonetheless, she was making progress. Her prototype of a safety pin key was turning slightly. Her finger was bleeding, but it was turning.

No!

It was turning from the other side!

Karen wrenched the safety pin out, crossed the room in two barefoot, silent steps, and flung herself on the cot, praying the big man wouldn't hear the squeak of the bed frame over the sound of the opening door.

It wasn't the big man. It was the Arab. He didn't seem to have noticed. He came in carrying a little black satchel that looked like a doctor's bag.

Karen's heart was already pounding from the close escape, but the black bag scared her more than anything. The Arab set it on the floor, knelt down next to it.

His cell phone rang.

Abdul-Hakim frowned, took it out, and checked caller ID. If it was Calvin Hancock, he'd have to take it.

It wasn't, but he had to take it anyway.

It was his contact on the Coast.

22

As far as the Santa Monica police were concerned, an abandoned Lexus near the airport was either catnip for car thieves, or part of a prearranged drug drop, so they had it towed in and searched for contraband. They got quite a surprise when they popped the trunk.

Abdul-Hakim mustered all the information he could before he called Calvin Hancock.

"This is unacceptable," Calvin said. "You're telling me a movie producer walks off the set, kills a hit man, and disappears?"

"We'll find him. The student's body was found a mile from the Santa Monica airport. We know Billy Barnett was on his way to the airport to borrow Peter Barrington's plane. Shortly before midnight that plane took off for Reno. It never got there. But we're not taking anything for granted. We're searching the airport in Reno, and the airports here."

"Are we sure he ever left?"

"He wasn't on the set today. He and his wife have a house, we're searching it now. The men on the job are thorough. And, yes, we're searching the airport in Santa Monica."

"What else?"

"We're searching hotel reservations, car rentals, plane, train, and bus tickets, any credit card use whatsoever in the name of Billy Barnett. He can't have disappeared into thin air."

"I'm pleased to hear it. So you tell me, then."

"What?"

"Where's Billy Barnett?"

23

Teddy Fay whizzed through the CIA website with an ease that had made him one of the most proficient agents in the history of the agency, as well as its greatest menace. In his twenty years outfitting agents for deep cover missions, Teddy had embraced each nuance with a delight usually reserved for computer nerds. In reaching new levels of efficiency, acquiring new weapons, activating and employing them in the hands of the agents he outfitted, Teddy was in effect playing a gigantic computer game.

And no one played it better.

Teddy did a search for subversive activity on the UCLA campus. Within minutes he was looking at a photograph of Alan Johnson, the young man who'd ambushed him in Peter's airplane hangar. Teddy had a name, could have searched for him that way, but he wanted to see if he'd find him through other channels. Alan Johnson was flagged for no less than four subversive organizations. Three were political fringe groups. One was suspected of having links to ISIS, but the links were rather tenuous. Not one single known ISIS member was confirmed.

Teddy did a search for known associates, but the kid was pretty much a loner. He'd been involved with two girls from campus, but neither had any political connections.

Teddy checked on terrorist activity in the D.C. area. The report was extensive. Since the assassination of the congressman, every top Al Qaeda official was rumored to be in town.

Teddy concerned himself with reports before the assassination. There were four Al Qaeda operatives in the area. Three of them Teddy knew, but none would have fired the shot or were capable of coordinating the kidnapping and the assassination, if indeed the two were connected. They surely must be — attacks on two conservative Republican members of Congress couldn't be coincidence. Had the CIA any inkling that the Speaker's daughter had been kidnapped, this website would explode. The chance of nothing leaking would be nil. The Speaker's daughter would be as good as dead.

No, the CIA knew nothing. The girl's fate

lay in the hands of Teddy, Holly, and a young woman barely old enough to vote. Okay, what next? Ordinarily he'd have known, but a lack of sleep was catching up with him.

On a whim, he looked up Lance Cabot. The director's home page was sparse, a brief bio listing training, positions, and titles. Any further information was coded and encrypted.

"Lance, you paranoid bastard," Teddy said. "What have you got to hide?"

He rolled up his sleeves and began breaking the code.

24

Holly Barker marveled at Kate's poise. Holly couldn't help watching the President during the briefing. No one in the room knew there'd been a kidnapping, yet here she was, conducting the meeting with a calm demeanor as if, aside from the fact that there'd been an assassination, nothing was wrong.

"All right," Kate said. "I realize it's very early, but what have we got? Lance?"

Holly suppressed a smile. Lance looked like a student who hadn't read the assignment and was hoping the teacher wouldn't call on him.

"We're canvassing for witnesses. Naturally, no one saw the shooting. We know where the shot was fired, from the rooftop across the street. A rifle cartridge shell is being processed even as we speak, not that there's much to tell until we have a rifle to match it up with. We're currently combing through security footage looking for anyone who could have smuggled a rifle in."

"With any success?"

"Too much. Assuming the rifle was one that could be broken down and carried in an attaché case, we have a few hundred suspects. We're sorting them out now."

"Who are we tracking who might be responsible?"

Lance rattled through the list of suspected Al Qaeda, ISIS, and Taliban agents. "With each passing moment it becomes less likely any of them were involved."

"Why?"

"Because no one has taken responsibility for it. With a terrorist attack of this sort, normally someone would. If there's no claim within the next hour, we would be inclined to look on any subsequent claim as false."

The FBI and Homeland Security reported in, but as Lance said, it was way too early and no one had anything concrete.

Holly Barker got back from the meeting to find Teddy Fay still online.

"What are you doing?"

"Requisitioning some equipment."

"In my name?"

"No, of course not."

"Surely not in yours."

"No, but agent Charles Dobson has a very important mission. We don't want to send our boys out ill-equipped."

"What is Charles Dobson getting?"

"Sorry. It's classified." Teddy swung away from the computer. "You don't have to tell me how your meeting went. I'm tracking no terrorist activity in the D.C. area yesterday. Today every top Al Qaeda agent not already romping with the eighty-two virgins is in town. No one's got anything, so everyone's making things up."

"That's about it," Holly said.

"How'd they react to the bullet?"

"You mean its being CIA? Lance didn't mention it."

"Why is Lance so paranoid?"

"What makes you say that?"

"I checked out his file. His encrypted, classified, eyes-only, super-secret file."

"What's in it?"

"Nothing. That's the point. He's got this totally secure file no one can get into, and he's afraid to put anything in it."

"You got into it."

Teddy waved that point away. "What's he afraid of?"

"You recall the incident when the plane carrying the sultan's twin sons was blown out of the sky just before it reached Dahai?"

The incident had set off an international firestorm. Only the highest ranking members of the CIA, FBI, and British Secret Service knew the true facts of the situation — that the twins had been integral participants in a plot to assassinate key figures in the US and UK. Stone Barrington had had a hand in foiling it.

"Sure," Teddy said. "Their neighbors in Yemen took credit for shooting down the plane. Some group calling itself Freedom for Dahai."

"Right. Those twins were sleeper cells responsible for a simultaneous attack against the prime minister of England and the president of the United States."

"I missed that tidbit."

"Everyone did. The attack was thwarted by a joint effort of British Secret Service and our CIA. Millie was involved, along with her friend in the FBI. We captured the twins before they could do any damage."

"So, Lance got them declared persona non grata, sent them home, and got his friends in Yemen to shoot them down before they got there." Teddy nodded. "Good move. It's what I would have done."

"Whether Lance actually did it or not, the

sultan holds him responsible."

"I can see how he would."

"Do you think that has anything to do with this?"

"Hell, no. But it's certainly interesting. So Lance is vulnerable. I suppose that means you and the President are, too."

"I may be. Kate is out of the loop."

"As I'm sure a thirteen-week congressional hearing would establish. I'd prefer to skip the process. Do you happen to know a Margo Sappington from the White House counsel's office?"

"Sounds familiar."

"Would she have an office in this building?"

"Let me check." Holly did a search. "Yes, she does."

"Great. Could you ask her to step in?"

Margo Sappington waited patiently in front of Holly Barker's desk until the national security advisor finished her phone call.

"You wished to see me?" she said, when Holly finally hung up.

"Yes. Thanks for stopping by."

"I'm surprised you have time for me in light of the assassination."

"That's what I'd like to talk to you about."

"Is there something I can help with?"

"There may be." Holly got up from her desk. "Let's go into the conference room."

Margo followed Holly through the door.

The massive oak table in the conference room could have seated sixteen. At the moment there was only one person sitting at it.

Teddy Fay didn't bother to get up. "Margo Sappington?" he said.

"Yes."

Teddy flipped open his credentials, slid them across the table. "Fred Walker, CIA."

"What's this all about?"

Teddy took his credentials back, slipped them into his pocket. "Please sit down."

Margo looked at Holly, then pulled out a chair and sat opposite Teddy. Holly sat next to her as if for support.

Teddy flipped open a file. "You were at Congressman Drexel's table at the state dinner last night?"

"Yes. But I doubt if I can help you, I didn't even speak to him."

"Were you seated next to him?"

"No, I was across the table from him."

"Who was seated next to him?"

"Some congressman or other. I don't recall."

"On his right or his left?"

"His left."

"And on the other side?"

"I didn't notice."

"So, you noticed who was on his left, but not who was on his right?"

"I wouldn't have noticed at all if he hadn't been shot. I'm trying my best to remember."

"Who was sitting next to you?"

"A congressman from Ohio and an attorney from New York."

"That would be Stone Barrington?"

"That's right."

"Did you know Stone Barrington was go-

124

ing to be sitting next to you?"

"I'm only an attorney in the White House counsel's office. I had no idea who I would be sitting next to. I was just happy to be asked."

Teddy referred to the file. "According to the original seating plan, Stone Barrington, the man you were sitting next to, was placed next to Congressman Drexel."

"Oh, for goodness' sakes."

"What?"

"Is that what this is all about? Look, I got to the dinner early, saw I was sitting between two stuffy married congressmen. I noticed Stone Barrington's place card, and though we'd never met, I'd heard of him, so I swapped places. It's just as well I did. Drexel was annoyed at Stone Barrington just for being there at all, so they wouldn't have enjoyed a pleasant dinner next to each other."

"You wound up leaving with Stone Barrington?"

"I didn't leave with him."

"But you went to his hotel room later last night?"

"That's none of your business."

Teddy set the wiretap device on the table in front of her. "That's when you planted this bug in Stone Barrington's cell phone."

"Oh, for goodness' sakes." Margo rolled her eyes. "You CIA guys are unbelievable. It's like the right hand doesn't know what the left hand is doing."

"What are you talking about?"

"Yes, of course I planted a bug in Stone Barrington's cell phone. That's what your colleague told me to do."

"What?"

"Your agent contacted me late yesterday afternoon when I was on my way home to change. He gave me the bug to plant, said there'd been a late addition to the dinner, Stone Barrington, an attorney from New York. I was to make sure I sat next to him, chat him up during dinner, and find an opportunity to bug his phone."

"Which you did?"

"That's right."

Teddy knew the answer to the next question. He just wanted to see if she'd tell the truth. "And that's why you went back to his hotel room and had sex with him. So you could bug his phone."

Margo flushed. "Actually . . ."

"Actually, what?"

"I managed to bug his phone during dinner."

Teddy gave Holly a look. She was trying to suppress her amusement.

126

"How'd you know how to bug a phone?" Teddy asked.

"The agent showed me. I wasn't very good at it, so he told me to take the phone to the ladies' room to do it. Later I'd pretend I just found it on the floor."

"How did you get ahold of the phone?"

"Picking Stone's pocket wasn't hard." Margo's eyes twinkled. "He was rather easy to distract."

"The agent who talked to you," Teddy said. "What did he look like?"

"Probably of Middle Eastern descent, clean-cut, good-looking."

"Middle Eastern?"

"Arab features. But Americanized, you know? He spoke perfect English, with little trace of an accent. And he was well-dressed. He looked like an agent."

"How'd you know he was CIA?"

"He had credentials."

26

Stone Barrington fished his cell phone out of his pocket. "Yes?"

"Are you in your hotel?"

"I am," Stone replied, recognizing the voice on the line.

"Walk east. Go in the first bar on your left and take a table in the back."

Five minutes later Stone walked into the bar. He had no trouble recognizing the man sitting at a table in the back as Teddy Fay, despite his Fred Walker persona.

Stone sat down across from him. "Who are you now?"

"Doesn't matter."

"Are we about done playing cops and robbers?"

"I certainly hope so. Let's see your phone."

Stone handed it over. Teddy slipped the back off, checked it out again.

"What did you want to tell me?"

"Holly just came from a national security briefing. The whole thing gets more and more complicated. Lance is holding out on the President, too."

"Lance knows about the kidnapping?"

"No. It turns out the shell from the sniper's rifle was CIA issue."

"Lance is withholding that from the President?"

"That's not the half of it. He thinks I fired the shot."

"Are you serious?"

"Only half. He called Holly to ask her. She pooh-poohed the idea."

"Are you sure?"

"I was in her office. She told him that Teddy Fay would never jeopardize his clean slate."

"He buy that?"

"He said so. Deep down inside I suspect he still thinks I did it."

"I happen to know you didn't."

"Thanks for your support."

"Well, it's not like I'd put it past you, but we happened to be having brunch at the time."

"That's right. The last time we talked it was just a kidnapping. Now we have an assassination."

"You think they're related?"

"Only if this is all about passing the veterans aid bill. I find that hard to believe."

"No kidding," Stone said. "So, is that all you've got?"

"You're disappointed I haven't found the girl yet? Well, I found out who bugged your phone."

"Really? Who?"

"Margo Sappington, just like I thought. She was a setup. She was told to get close to you and plant the bug. I'm sorry to deflate your ego, but she didn't just fall for your manly charm. She was programmed by a man posing as a CIA agent."

"Any description?"

"Not good enough to work with. Middle Eastern features, clean-cut, looked like an agent. I'll track him down when I've had some sleep. Right now I can hardly think straight."

Stone frowned. "What does any of this have to do with the missing girl?"

Teddy shrugged. "I don't know yet."

27

Karen had to get out of there fast before the Arab came back with his doctor bag. She had no idea what the phone call was that saved her, but she couldn't count on it happening again.

The big man came in with her lunch, a sandwich on a plastic plate. He set it on the floor and went out. Karen didn't have to look at it to know what it was. Processed cheese with mayonnaise on white bread.

Karen ignored her lunch, went to the door. There was no sound from the other side. The big man was gone. She took out the safety pin. She'd bent it wrenching it out of the door. She folded it back into the shape that had almost worked before. She exhaled nervously, and fitted it into the keyhole.

It wouldn't go. Something was blocking it.

Karen pulled it out, knelt down, and

peered through the keyhole, trying to see what the problem was.

She couldn't see a thing. They'd plugged the hole. Why? Just to keep her from looking? If so, what didn't they want her to see?

Or were they on to her? Had they plugged the hole so she couldn't try to pick the lock?

Karen took the fully straightened pin and thrust the pointed end into the keyhole. She immediately hit the obstruction. She poked around at it, and realized what it was.

The key!

The big man had left the key in the lock. Now if she could just turn it from the inside.

She poked at the key with the point of the safety pin. But it was hopeless. She couldn't get a purchase to turn the key. And she couldn't grab it with the other end of the pin.

What could she possibly do?

She needed a newspaper. If she had a newspaper she could slide it under the door, poke the key out so it fell on the paper, and then pull it back. But they weren't going to give her a newspaper. She'd asked, but they refused. Probably didn't want her to know what was going on. It wasn't that they didn't want her to read. After all, they gave her a book.

All right. What could she do with a book?

28

Teddy stopped in at the CIA headquarters to pick up the equipment he'd requisitioned online under the name of Charles Dobson. He flashed Dobson's ID and looked appropriately bored while the agent verified the card and double-checked the provisions. Naturally they checked out. Teddy had uploaded agent Dobson's service record to the CIA mainframe while he was on Holly's computer. And Charles Dobson looked enough like Fred Walker that the ID photo wasn't hard to match. A slightly different hairstyle did the trick.

Minutes later Teddy was out the door with four handguns, a sniper rifle, a generous supply of ammunition, half a dozen burner phones, and a few choice burglar tools, such as heavy-duty bolt cutters.

Teddy went back to the second-rate hotel he'd checked into earlier that morning. Not that he couldn't afford a first-rate hotel, he just didn't want that kind of attention. No one gave a damn about him here. As long as he had his room key, he could activate the elevator. He rode up to the eighth floor and let himself into his room.

Teddy stashed the equipment under the bed, took out one of the burner phones, and called Betsy on her cell. "Hi, honey. I don't have much time to talk."

That was their code. When Betsy heard that, she knew to give no specific information, just make generic responses and wait for her cue.

"I tried to call you before," Teddy said, "but it's crunch time and I'm very busy. I won't have time to watch TV, so remember to set the DVR."

"You got it."

Betsy hung up the phone with a sense of foreboding. There were no shows Teddy wanted her to DVR. He'd been trying to give her a message.

Before she had time to think about it, a production assistant ran up to summon her back to the movie set.

Today the movie crew was shooting on the sound stage at Centurion Studios. Betsy tapped Peter on the arm. "I gotta run back to the office." He nodded, and she went out the door.

Peter's office was at the other end of the lot. Betsy could have taken a golf cart, but she always walked so she did now. There was no reason to make anyone think she was in a rush.

Betsy hurried into Peter's office, grabbed the remote, flicked on the TV. It was tuned to ESPN. Betsy shook her head, clicked the remote, and changed the channel.

It was still breaking news on MSNBC: **CONGRESSMAN ASSASSINATED.**

Betsy sucked in her breath.

Good God, Teddy. What have you done now?

29

Karen took the paperback thriller, opened it in the middle, put it facedown on the floor, and broke the spine. She flipped a few pages and smashed the spine again. She picked up the book, grabbed the pages, and slowly, carefully tore them out.

They came out attached by the glue from the spine. She carefully separated two pages from the bunch. She opened them up in the middle and flattened them out. The pages held. She set them aside, and did it again. She tore out a dozen more attached pages.

Now, if she just had a way to stick them together. Tape, or glue, or staples. Anything.

The room had clearly been used as a workroom. The old metal sink was stained with bleach and floor wax and shellac and varnish and whatever else had been dumped into it over the years. One blue paint smear was fairly thick and relatively fresh. It appeared to be enamel paint. It gave when Karen picked at it.

Karen dumped the sandwich on the floor and used the edge of the plastic plate to scrape some paint off the sink. She diluted it with water, mushed it around with her fingertips. After several minutes it felt slightly sticky.

It was poor glue at best, but it would have to do. Karen laid two pages on the floor side by side and smeared a half-inch line of paint down the edge of one. She overlapped the other, then leaned all her weight on them, pressing them together against the floor as hard as she could. She relaxed the pressure, sat back on her heels to evaluate her work. It wasn't big enough, of course, she'd have to add to it, but it would tell her if her paint-glue would hold.

It wouldn't.

The pages came apart as soon as she tried to tug them across the floor. And that was without the added weight of the key. She needed better glue.

Karen had been so engrossed in her task she'd neglected to clean up. The big man would be coming in to get the plate. There was paint on the edge of it. And paint on her hands. And the pages from the book were lying on the floor.

Karen gathered up the pages and shoved

them back in the book. She washed her hands and washed the plate. The plate fared better. When she was done, there was just a trace of paint on the edge, barely detectable. Her hands would not pass a close inspection.

She put the sandwich on the plate. She knew she should eat it, or the big man would wonder why, might think she was sick. Then the Arab would come back with his doctor bag and try to cure her. She shivered at the thought.

It didn't matter that she had no appetite. She had to choke down the sandwich.

Karen blinked.

The cheese and mayonnaise sandwich.

Mayonnaise.

It worked. The mayonnaise held. The two pages passed the tug test. Cursing herself for wasting so much time with the paint, Karen pasted pages together into a single sheet. It was a rectangle, three pages wide by two pages deep. It should be enough. If only the key didn't bounce sideways, or too far away from the door.

Karen knelt down and started to slide her makeshift sheet of paper under the door, just below the key.

The key turned in the lock!

Karen whisked the paper away from the door, thrust it under the mattress, and threw herself facedown on the cot.

The door opened and he came in. She snuck a peek. To her relief, it was the big man. He scowled at her uneaten mangled sandwich, but he didn't say anything, he just picked up the plate and went out.

She waited a minute to make sure he was gone. Then she retrieved the paper from under the mattress. It was crushed and torn. All the pages were separated. And the big man had taken the sandwich, so there was no mayonnaise to fix it.

It wouldn't have mattered.

He'd also taken the key.

30

Millie Martindale had no problem recognizing Karen Blaine's boyfriend from the pictures on her Facebook page. According to several girls in the dorm with whom she'd spoken earlier, Karen had just broken up with the young man, and he wasn't taking it well. Millie found him slumped over a beer in the college bar. She slid in next to him and said, "Hi."

He took no notice. He might not have heard her.

"Are you Jason?"

He looked up then. "Who are you?"

"I'm a friend of Karen's."

He winced as if her name hurt. "Oh, come on."

"We were supposed to go away for the weekend. She didn't show."

"So?"

"I haven't seen her since. I'm worried about her."

He shrugged, and took a sip of his beer.

"I'm sorry to bother you. I know you guys broke up."

"Who told you that?"

"The girls at the dorm. Look, I know how you feel. Believe me, I've been there. But it's not the end of the world. And it doesn't mean she won't change her mind."

"There's another guy!"

He said it loud. Heads turned. The bartender looked over. Millie waited for him to look away and said, "How do you know?"

Jason said nothing, stared at his glass.

"Did she tell you there's another guy?"

"I saw him!"

He said it loud again. This time the bartender said, "You wanna keep it down?"

Millie put up her hand and nodded compliance to the bartender. She turned back to Jason. "You saw him?" she said. She tried not to appear too eager. "What did he look like?"

"I didn't get a good look. But he was way too old for her, with his fancy clothes and big SUV."

"You saw them together?"

"He picked her up at the dorm."

"Did he bring her back?"

"What, you think I waited there all night? She went out with him, I haven't seen her

141

since. Some long date."

"I'm sorry."

"When she comes back she'll lie about it. Right to my face, she'll lie about it. But I've got pictures."

Millie's pulse leaped. "Pictures?"

"I took pictures with my cell phone."

"You got pictures of her with the guy?"

"That's right."

"That's smart. Let me see."

Jason was wearing blue jeans and a sports shirt. He fished in his pockets and came out with a cell phone. In his drunken state he had trouble switching it on.

Jason's photos weren't great. He'd apparently taken care not to let Karen's boyfriend see him. As a result, they were shot from a distance and tended to feature the couple's backs. And the man was mostly in the shadows. Still, one or two might be good enough to use.

Millie bought Jason a beer and managed to distract his attention while she slipped the cell phone under a napkin on the bar. Then she simply waited him out. Half a beer later he got up and headed for the men's room. She grabbed the cell phone, called up the pictures, and spent several agonizing seconds figuring out how to send them. Working feverishly, she forwarded them to her own phone.

They weren't sending. What was it with these phones? Sometimes they were instantaneous, sometimes they got hung up. She didn't have time to reboot and resend. The pictures just didn't go.

They went. The phone flashed, and the screen returned to normal. Millie put down the phone just as Jason came back.

Millie smiled and pointed.

"Left your cell phone on the bar."

31

Karen was running out of options. The safety pin wasn't strong enough to turn in the lock. The key was gone. The paper was shredded by the bedsprings.

The bedspring. She'd all but given up on the bedspring, just as she'd all but given up on the safety pin.

And yet.

Karen flipped up the mattress, retrieved her spring. She took the safety pin and tried to put them together. The wire of the spring was just the right size to fit in the clasp of the pin. It just wasn't the right shape. No matter. Karen could bend the wire.

After several abortive attempts Karen managed to fit the wire snugly into the clasp of the pin. It would be hard to hold it there, but she twisted the other end of the pin around the spring with the point sticking out.

Karen held her breath and fitted the

makeshift key into the lock. She gripped it tight and turned. The point of the pin went into her finger, gave her some purchase. She eased the key in and out, trying to find the place where the tumblers would turn.

It was horribly frustrating. It was almost working. The key would move slightly, then it would slip. Her finger was torn and bleeding. She kept removing the key and making adjustments. Some made it better, some made it worse. None made it open. She kept on trying.

Abdul-Hakim looked up from the couch. "It's time to go."

The big man was annoyed. He was watching a game show on TV in the adjoining room, and he was keeping it low like he'd been told, and he ought to be allowed to watch it. But no, the guy decides out of the blue it's time to go, and now isn't soon enough.

"Uh-huh," he said without moving.

"Go get the girl."

The contestant on TV was going for the showcase. "Just a minute."

"Now!" Abdul-Hakim said it in no uncertain terms.

The big man sighed and heaved himself out of his chair.

■ ■ ■ ■

The lock clicked open.

Karen couldn't believe it. She was sure they'd opened it from the other side, and she sprang back onto the cot. But no one came in. She got up, went to the door, and listened. She heard nothing. She tried the knob. It turned and the door opened.

She couldn't see a thing. There were no lights. Karen stood for a moment and let her eyes grow accustomed to the dark.

Overhead pipes. Heating ducts. A concrete floor.

She was in a basement, but it wasn't pitch-dark. There was a trace of light. Where was it coming from? Karen glanced around.

There were two small windows near the top of the far wall. They'd been painted black, but some light was leaking in. They didn't look big enough to climb through. There were some crates she could climb on, but they didn't look high enough.

Karen looked around frantically, but couldn't see anything useful. Just a couple of lawn chairs and a lawn mower.

She paused. A lawn mower!

There must be a door to the outside!

Karen started across the room and —

Her face fell.

No one was using the lawn mower. It had been brought down there and junked. It was actually missing a wheel.

Suddenly a shaft of light split the darkness of the cellar. Karen jumped back into the shadows.

The big man came down the cellar stairs. Two steps down he reached out, grabbed a string, and pulled on an overhead light. It was a hundred-watt bare bulb, and it lit up the shadows. Karen was sure he could see her. She shrunk back, willed herself to be very small.

The big man clumped down the stairs and plodded across the cellar toward her room. He turned the corner and was out of sight in the alcove in front of the door.

Should she risk trying for the stairs?

She'd never make it. He was at the door. He had only to push it open and he'd be back.

But there was no place to hide, and time was running out.

Why wasn't he back?

The big man pulled the skeleton key out of his pocket, fitted it in the keyhole, and unlocked the door. He turned the knob and pushed.

It didn't open.

He frowned. How was that possible? The door should be open.

He turned the knob and pushed the door again.

No. It was still locked.

He looked at the skeleton key. Could it be the wrong one? Even he knew that was a dumb idea. The key had turned, but the door was locked. It didn't make any sense.

He stuck the key back in and turned it.

The lock clicked open.

She should have gone. It was taking longer than she thought. She should go now.

Karen scrunched backward into the shadow.

The big man exploded around the corner and thundered down on her.

Karen was trapped. She turned to meet her fate.

The big man rushed by her and stormed up the stairs.

Karen couldn't believe it. She crawled out, ran to the stairs, and listened. She heard nothing. That was odd. She'd expected to hear the big man raise the alarm, but he hadn't.

Karen crept up the stairs. The door at the top was open. She stuck her head out, looked around.

The cellar door was at one end of a long, narrow hallway.

At the other end was the front door.

Karen listened, trying to determine where the big man had gone. She could hear footsteps overhead. He was searching the upstairs rooms.

Karen started down the hall.

To the right was the door to the kitchen, but it had no exterior door. She kept going, past the stairs to the second floor. Now the big man couldn't come down and cut her off. She was almost there. Just the living room and the foyer to go.

Karen's eyes were on the knob of the bolt lock on the front door. She could turn it with her left hand while her right hand turned the doorknob. A matter of seconds. The big man couldn't stop her.

Karen froze.

Through the door to the living room she could see the Arab was on the couch, his black doctor's bag on the coffee table in front of him.

Karen shrunk back in alarm. The front door was a tantalizing fifteen feet away, but there was no way she could reach it now.

Overhead the footsteps got louder.

The big man was coming back down the stairs.

Karen was trapped. She couldn't go forward, and she couldn't go back.

There was a coat closet on her left. Karen pulled the door open and ducked inside.

"She's gone!"

Abdul-Hakim sprang to his feet. "What?"

"She's not there!"

"You left the door unlocked?"

"Hell, no!"

"Then how did she get out?"

"I don't know!"

Abdul-Hakim was sure he didn't. The big man never knew. "Search the house."

"I did."

"Before you told me?" Abdul-Hakim said ominously. "How long has she been out?"

"I don't know."

"Check if the doors are locked."

"They open from the inside."

"They don't lock from the *outside*. If the dead bolt's on, she didn't use it. Search the house."

"I told you. I searched the house."

"Search it again. Check the closets."

Karen peered out from the coat closet. The Arab was guarding the front door. She

150

shrunk back in again.

She was trapped. The Arab would see her the moment she came out, and the big man's search wouldn't take long. Any minute he'd wrench the door open, and that would be that.

Footsteps thundered down the hall.

Karen peered out the tiniest crack.

And here he came, straight at her.

He reached for the doorknob.

Karen caught him by surprise. She threw all her weight against the door, slamming him into the wall. Before he could react she sprang from the closet and sprinted up the stairs, just ahead of the Arab and the big man.

Karen raced down the hall. There was a bathroom at the other end. She dashed in, slammed the door, and locked it just as the big man hit it full force. The door splintered but held.

The bathroom had a window, small but she could fit. Karen hopped up on the toilet, grabbed the bottom half and heaved. The window slid open, not all the way, but enough.

The door splintered again. The doorknob was nearly broken off.

Karen stuck her head and arms out the window and began to shimmy through.

There came a tremendous splintering of wood.

Karen felt the hands on her legs, yanking her away from freedom. She crashed to the floor under the weight of the big man and all the breath was knocked out of her.

From somewhere she could hear the voice of the Arab saying, "Bad girl."

Then she felt the prick of a hypodermic needle, and everything went dark.

32

When shooting wrapped for the day, Betsy snuck away and went home. Since Teddy left she'd been a good girl and followed Peter and Ben back and forth to work, but enough was enough. She needed a change of clothes, just in and out. She wouldn't pack a suitcase, just throw a few things into a grocery bag.

At least she told herself that was the reason. But if the truth be told, she didn't know if Teddy had stopped by the house before he left. If he had, she was hoping there'd be some clue as to what he was doing, how he was connected to what was going on.

Betsy knew Teddy wouldn't like what she was doing. But she was a big girl. She'd taken care of herself in Vegas for years, and she could take care of herself now. It was not like she was some babe in the woods.

Betsy drove by the house slowly, checked

the place out. There were no cars in the street, no cars parked in the vicinity. The car in Mr. Rydell's driveway belonged to the owner.

Betsy was not going to park blocks away and walk in. It was her house. She'd park in the driveway, bold as brass. Grab the clothes and check for clues, more or less at the same time.

Betsy unlocked the front door. She glanced over her shoulder to make sure no one was taking an interest in her. No one was.

Betsy pushed the door open and gasped.

The place had been wrecked.

33

Stone Barrington grabbed his cell phone off the end table and checked caller ID. It was Peter. Stone pressed the button, clicked it on. "Hi, Peter. How's the filming going?"

"Slowed up a little bit. Someone trashed my assistant's house and the police were around asking lots of questions."

"Everything all right now?"

"Oh, sure. It's just vandalism, nobody was injured."

"Well, that's good. Sorry to hear you got troubles. You must not have time to talk. Listen. Take care of business, I'll call you another time."

Stone got off the phone.

Peter had been discreet, not mentioning any names, but he'd gotten the message across. Something needed to be done.

Stone went out to a pay phone and called Teddy.

"I told you not to call me."

"I'm at a pay phone."

"I'm surprised you found one. What's up?"

Stone told him. Teddy wanted to go home.

"You can't."

"I know."

"Let me handle this for you."

"How?"

"Mike Freeman."

Teddy considered. "Total coverage?"

"Total."

Teddy exhaled in frustration. "All right. Thanks."

Stone went back to his room and called Mike Freeman at Security Services.

"Hi, Stone," Mike said. "Calling to thank me for the cell phone? Of course a lot's happened since."

"Tell me about it."

"Is this about the assassination?"

"I have a personal matter, Mike. I was hoping you could help me out."

"This isn't business?"

"Actually, it is. I find myself in the market for some security services. I can't think of a better person to call."

"Frankly, I can't either. What's up?"

"My son Peter's run into a bit of a snag."

"Didn't he just get married?"

"Not that type of problem, Mike. His assistant on the movie crew just had her house broken into."

"Anyone hurt?"

"No."

"Anything taken?"

"Not that she can tell. But the place was trashed."

"That's not good."

"No kidding. My son's putting her up for the time being, but he's a newlywed, and I'm sure playing bodyguard wasn't high on his wish list."

"I can imagine."

"I want complete coverage. But surreptitious. Unobtrusive."

"You won't be needing a camera in the bedroom. I quite understand."

"There's another honeymoon couple. Dino's son, Ben, just got married also. Ben and Peter are making a movie out there. Peter's directing, Ben's running the studio. There's a lot going on. We're not necessarily talking home invasion."

"You want my men to get jobs as extras in the movie?"

"No, and if they're starstruck and distracted I will not be amused."

"My men are pros."

"Men are men. You haven't seen some of these actresses."

"I'll read them the riot act," Mike said. "Tell me, this assistant you speak of. Would that be anyone in particular?"

"She's the wife of a mutual friend."

"Ah. This begins to make sense. And you don't want your son to get caught in the crossfire."

"Something like that. I was sort of hoping for the survival of the assistant, too."

"I didn't mean to give you the impression I wasn't. All right, I'll give it my highest priority."

"I'm glad to hear it. But you have to understand this job's important to me. I would really like *personal* coverage."

"What do you mean?"

"How'd you like a vacation in sunny L.A.?"

34

Karen came to in the back of the van. Not the one the man had driven up to her dorm — that had been an SUV. This was a service van, and she was bumping along on the metal floor. It was the jouncing that had woken her.

She tried to stand up and fell on her face. Her hands and feet were tied. Why? Didn't the door lock? Could it be opened from inside? Her pulse leaped.

Was this her chance?

Karen struggled to her feet. It wasn't easy. Her hands were tied behind her, so she couldn't use them to push up.

There were no windows in the van. There were curtained rear windows, with the blinds just loose enough to let in the tiniest sliver of light. She wobbled over there, supporting herself against the side, praying she wouldn't fall, afraid she'd never get up again, and tried to move the curtain with her nose. She pushed it aside but there was nothing to see. The only light was from the headlights shining in the opposite direction. Behind the van there was only darkness, a void.

That couldn't be right. There had to be some sort of light. Was there another curtain beyond the one she was looking behind? No, then the light from the headlights wouldn't show. The van was simply driving where there were no lights.

And where the road was bumpy. It was all she could do just to stand.

The van pulled to a stop in the middle of nowhere and she felt an icy rush of fear. Was this where it was going to happen?

An instinct for survival told her she shouldn't be found standing. She threw herself to the floor of the van, forced herself not to cry out as she banged her head.

The rear door opened. She kept her eyes closed. The big man dragged her out of the van, picked her up in his arms. He carried her up a couple of steps. Karen heard the squeak of a door.

He banged her head going in. He didn't seem to notice, just kept going.

He sat her down on what seemed like a mattress. Only he'd lowered her too far for her to be on a bed. She heard the floorboards squeak. The big man was going away.

She risked opening her eyes.

She was on a mattress on the floor in a tiny room of what appeared to be a cabin. There was a small window in the back wall, but it was too high for her to see out. There was a door on the opposite wall, or at least a doorway. A tattered sheet had been hung from the top of it to form a curtain. The room was bare except for the mattress on the floor.

Where the hell was she?

And why had they brought her here?

35

Teddy couldn't get over the pictures on Millie's phone.

"He photographed the guy?" Teddy said. "It's a brave new world. In my day, if you wanted to confront your significant other with infidelity, you hired a private eye."

"Are you suggesting that's better or worse?" Holly said.

"Well, it's certainly different. All right, let's see what we've got here."

Millie scrolled through the pictures on the phone.

"This is incredibly disappointing," Teddy said.

"I know."

"The guy's three-quarters profile and he's in the dark."

"The boyfriend was afraid to get any closer."

"Could he see any better? Can he describe the guy at all?"

Millie shook her head. "He couldn't. Of course, he was drunk when I met him and I couldn't push the point, but I really don't think he knows."

"What you see is what you get," Teddy said. He scrolled through the photos, chose the one with the best angle. "All right, let's see if we can make this any better."

Teddy sat down at Holly's computer and loaded the picture into Photoshop. He cropped the man's head, enlarged it, and played with the color and contrast. A face emerged from the shadows.

Millie sucked in her breath. "Look!"

"Nicely done," Holly said. "You think it's our guy?"

"Let's find out. Millie, that's all for now. On your way out, call Margo Sappington in the White House counsel's office and ask her to drop by, would you?"

Margo wasn't happy to be called back. "I told you everything I know," she protested when Holly ushered her into the conference room.

"I'm sure you did," Teddy said. He slid a copy of the photo across the table. "Do you recognize the man in the picture?"

Margo studied it and frowned. "It's a bad shot."

"Yes, it is."

"Are you asking if this is the agent who spoke to me?"

"Is he?" Holly said.

"He could be. Like I said, it's a bad shot."

Holly looked at Teddy. He nodded.

"Okay, thanks for coming in," Holly said.

"That's all you wanted?"

"That's all."

Margo went out.

"So, what now?" Holly said.

Teddy took a breath. "All right. We know Margo Sappington bugged Stone Barrington's phone. We don't know who told her to do it."

"An Arab-looking guy posing as a CIA agent," Holly said. "Most likely the guy in the picture."

"Right. The question is, how did the bogus agent know Stone would be at Margo's table?"

"Aren't there several possibilities?"

"Actually, no. Stone didn't know he was going until that very afternoon. He was summoned to the dinner by the President's chief of staff, Ann Keaton."

"It wasn't her."

"Are you sure?"

"She's a personal friend of Stone Barrington, and fiercely loyal to the President. She wouldn't have told anyone."

"She had to tell the tailor who made his suit."

"She had to tell him Stone's measurements. She would not have told him what table he was sitting at, so he couldn't have tipped the phony agent off to get Margo Sappington to plant the bug."

Holly's intercom buzzed. She picked up the phone. "Yes?"

"Lance Cabot is here to see you."

"Just a moment." Holly covered the mouthpiece. "Lance is here."

"Oops," Teddy said.

"He won't be long. Wait in the conference room."

Teddy slipped through the door.

Holly uncovered the phone and said, "Send him in."

Lance came in with a manila folder. He smiled. "Is that payback, Holly?"

"What?"

"Making me wait."

"Thirty seconds," Holly said.

"It's symbolic."

"What's up, Lance?"

"We got the shooter."

Holly raised her eyebrows. "What!"

"Well, we don't have him, but we think we've identified him."

Lance took a photograph out of the folder,

passed it over. The CIA had gotten it right. It was a picture of the man who was the actual shooter.

"This gentleman here. We're running facial recognition on him. So far we don't have a match."

"What makes you think he's the shooter?"

"This picture was taken from the surveillance video of the building where the shot was fired. He took the elevator up to the nineteenth floor at nine-fifteen that morning. He took the elevator down from the *eighteenth* floor at one-oh-five. The building is twenty-one stories high. We figure at nine-fifteen he got off at nineteen, slipped through the fire door, and took the service stairs up two flights so as not to be seen getting off on the floor with access to the roof. We figure after the shooting he lost track on the stairs and went down an extra flight."

"Is there any company with offices on both floors?"

"No. And he didn't take an elevator from one floor to the other."

"That's a good deduction. Did they have his name at security?"

"No. The guards at the desk make you present photo ID. If your face matches the face on the ID, they let you in."

"They don't keep written records?"

"No." The inflection in Lance's voice showed what he thought of that practice.

"It's just an office building, Lance, with no government affiliation."

"Yes, I know. It's just frustrating."

"What are you going to do with the photo?"

"We're going to let the D.C. police put it out as a person of interest they'd like to question."

"Why not put out a general alert?"

"We don't want to cause unnecessary panic. Though we suspect terrorism, we haven't yet discovered this man's identity or affiliations. If we basically declare that the assassination was a terrorist attack, the populace will wonder when the next one is coming."

"Do you think there's more to come?"

Lance looked grim. "Given what we know, it seems a safe assumption."

"You want to tell me what this guy would be doing with a CIA shell?"

"No. And I'm glad I don't have to be telling anybody else."

Lance smiled, and went out.

Teddy came out of the conference room. He picked up the photo and could see immediately it wasn't the same man they'd

167

identified in the photo from Karen's ex-boyfriend. "So. Another terrorist. I wonder what Lance would think if he knew we had one, too."

"I'm surprised facial recognition didn't work," Holly said. "This shot is certainly clear enough."

"These guys aren't mainstream, that's been clear from the start."

"So who are they?"

"And why in the world would they care about some bill in Congress?"

"It's a veterans aid bill," Holly said. "Maybe they're disgruntled vets."

"Disgruntled Middle Eastern terrorist vets? Trying to pass a bill? What the hell is that all about?" Teddy shook his head. "Can you get someone in here who knows something about Congress?"

36

Teddy frowned. "Who is this man?"

"Sam Snyder," Holly said. "He's a Democratic congressman from Maryland, and a personal friend of the President. He should know as much as anyone about the workings of Congress."

"Including why they'd be important to Middle Eastern terrorists?"

"Let's not hope for miracles."

Holly's phone rang. She answered, said, "Show him in," and hung up. "He's here."

"I should probably be seated at the conference table," Teddy said. "I don't know why it makes me look more official, but it does."

Teddy went into the conference room and sat down. Moments later Holly ushered Sam Snyder into the room.

Teddy sized up the elderly congressman, and figured him for friendly and verbose. He was right on both counts. Just the introductions threatened to bore Teddy to distraction. He managed to cut the old man short and urge him toward the point.

"I've never understood the workings of Congress," Teddy said, "and I appreciate your expertise. The veterans aid bill, for instance. What can you tell me about that?"

"Do you have all afternoon?" Sam Snyder said. His eyes twinkled. "You want to know the effect of the assassination on the veterans aid bill."

Teddy smiled. "Why do you say that?"

"Why else would you bring me here? You're wondering if I have any insights, being a friend of the President. I know Kate, and she isn't thinking in those terms. She's horrified by the death of Congressman Drexel. She'll deal with it, of course, but she's not glorying in the fact that the death of a Republican congressman makes it easier for the clean bill to pass."

"It does, doesn't it?" Teddy said.

"But of course. Congressman Drexel was one of the chief opponents of the bill."

"With him out of the way, will it pass?"

"The chances are certainly better. It really depends on what Speaker Blaine does. You know he's been meeting with the President. That's a very hopeful sign."

"What would happen if he came out in favor of the bill?"

"It's hard to say now. Congressman Drexel would have leaped into the breach, mounted a countercharge. With him gone, Congressman Herman Foster might step up, but he's a lesser light. The bill would have a strong chance of passing."

"I see."

"But it can't be the reason for the assassination. Why would the terrorists care about the bill? The one thing can't have anything to do with the other."

"He's absolutely right," Teddy said, after Sam Snyder had finally made a lengthy exit. "Why would the terrorists care if the bill passed or not? On the other hand, it's all the kidnappers seem to want. By rights, the kidnapping and the assassination shouldn't be connected at all."

"Except the kidnapper's Middle Eastern."

"Let's not fall into a racial profiling trap. They're both Middle Eastern. That doesn't mean they're working together."

"It would be nice to be able to prove they're not."

"I'd be happy either way," Teddy said. "It's not knowing that's driving me crazy."

37

The bell over the door chimed as Teddy entered the secondhand bookstore. He closed the door behind him and squinted in the near dark. It was a dusty, musty place, the type where old paperbacks that could be had four for a dollar on the city sidewalk were packed in plastic sleeves and went for five, ten, or even twenty bucks apiece. The type of store where a tattered volume of worthless text sat side by side with a priceless signed first edition of an early Ernest Hemingway.

Teddy pawed through a stack of books, waiting for the shopkeeper to emerge from the back.

The owner, a little old man named Saul, had greedy eyes. He sized Teddy up, said, "What can I do for you?"

"I'd like a first edition of *The Maltese Falcon.*"

Saul practically salivated. His look became

shrewd. "How much are you willing to pay?"

"Depends on the condition."

"But of course."

"Do you have one?"

"You have to understand. No one has a copy of a first edition of *The Maltese Falcon* lying around. But I can make a few calls and facilitate the transaction. If my shop were full of rare books, I would be robbed. So my shop is not full of rare books. My shop is full of books that are not worth stealing."

Saul realized he'd gone too far. "I don't mean they're not worth stealing. I mean they would have to be stolen in bulk to generate the type of revenue a rare book such as you mention would bring. How soon do you need the book?"

"Actually, I have some time. There's something else I need right away."

"What's that?"

"CIA credentials."

Saul's eyes narrowed. "Who are you?"

"You don't know me, Saul? Good."

"Teddy?" Saul was amazed. "I thought you were dead."

"Good thinking. Keep thinking that and we'll have no problem."

"I don't understand."

"You're a smart man, Saul. You'll figure it out."

Teddy and Saul went way back. Teddy had stepped in and saved Saul's skin when the little forger was trapped between an irate client on the one hand and the U.S. government on the other. The solution Teddy came up with would have done justice to a Solomon. Saul had paid him back by teaching him some of the techniques Teddy had put to good use in the course of his checkered career.

Saul sized Teddy up. "You want credentials? Of course you don't want credentials, you could make them yourself. You wouldn't come to me unless you had no access to the equipment, a position you would not place yourself in, unless you were in trouble. In which case you would not be here in D.C., because you're dead and you'd like to stay dead. So what do you really want?"

"Information."

Saul raised his hands, grimaced. "This is not what I sell. I would not stay in business long if my transactions weren't secure. How would you like it if I made you a passport for two thousand dollars and sold that information for five? You would not like it, and you would be inclined to let me know of your displeasure."

"How old are you, Saul?"

"Eighty-nine."

"Like to make ninety?"

"Teddy. We're friends. We go way back. I help you, you help me, it is a nice arrangement. I thought that arrangement had reached a natural conclusion. I was obviously misinformed. I am delighted you wish to renew our friendship. Please, how can I be of assistance to you?"

"Tell me about the CIA credentials."

"The ones you don't wish to buy?"

"The ones you already made, recently. Assuming you made only one. Or did you make more?"

"No, no. Just the one."

"Who did you make them for?"

"I don't know."

"That's less than helpful, Saul. That's not the answer of a friend."

"I know the name on the credentials, but I doubt if it's his."

"What would that be?"

"Martin Stark."

"Martin Stark?"

"Yes."

"So you immediately traced the name to see if there was a Martin Stark of his description, and, if so, if there was anything in his background to be worth some

175

money."

"Teddy. Would I do that?"

"I know you would. I'm asking if you did."

"There is no Martin Stark. That's why I feel confident telling you I don't know him."

"So. When you made the ID for him, did he give you a photo, or did you take one?"

"He had a photo."

"Did you make a copy?"

"I tried. He watched me too closely."

"What did he look like?"

"Clean-cut. Middle Eastern features. Well-dressed. Could easily pass for CIA. He had that cold, brusque manner, like he expected people to do what he said."

"Is that how you see us, Saul?"

"No reason to get huffy. That's not you anymore. You quit."

Teddy slid the photo of the man with the SUV across the counter. "Is this him?"

Saul peered at it, shrugged. "Could be. It's hard to tell from that picture."

Teddy picked it up and put down the photo of Lance's shooter suspect. "How about him?"

Saul picked it up. His hand trembled. He put it down and shook his head. "Wasn't him."

"Have you seen this man before?"

"No, I haven't."

"Are you sure, Saul?"

"This man was never in my shop. Of that I'm sure. It was probably the other one."

"Uh-huh. Do you know who this man is?"

"Is he the shooter?"

"Why do you say that, Saul?"

"Teddy. It's me, Saul. You think I don't know a surveillance video photo when I see one?"

"He's a person of interest, Saul. I'd like to know more about him. Are you sure you've never seen him before?"

"Teddy, I swear."

"Don't make me cross-examine you, Saul. The photo shook you. Have you ever seen this man's *photo* before?"

Saul sighed. All the resistance seemed to ooze out of him. "The man who was in my shop. He gave me this man's ID photo."

"You made *two* CIA credentials?"

"No."

"What did you make?"

"A driver's license."

"I see. So ever since the shooting you've been sweating bricks. If you didn't know everything there was to know about this man then, I'll bet you moved heaven and earth to find out."

"There's nothing to find. Believe me, I tried."

"What's his name?"

"The name on the driver's license was Nehan Othman. But it's not his name."

"How do you know?"

"If it was his own name, he wouldn't need me. He could simply get a driver's license."

"Unless he couldn't drive."

"I suppose. Still, it is not as easy to get a license for a man who doesn't exist." Saul laughed. "As if *I* should be telling *you.*"

"But you checked it anyway?"

"Of course. There is no one by that name."

"No, there wouldn't be."

"Are you sure he is the shooter?"

"It looks like it."

"I'm sorry if I helped him in any way." Saul shrugged. "But how was I to know?"

Teddy shook his head. "I'm sure it helps you to believe that."

38

Speaker Blaine was determined. He had spent the day steeling himself for what he had to do. What Stone Barrington said made good sense: he had to demand proof of life. He had to know one way or another whether his daughter was alive. By rights she had to be. If she wasn't, they got nothing. They had to prove she was.

His cell phone rang. He jumped at the sound. He had left it out on the table so he wouldn't have to fumble for it in his pocket. The ring echoed loudly in the silence. He snatched it up, clicked it on.

"Yes?" he said breathlessly.

It was the voice he'd come to dread. "You must not care about your daughter."

The demands he had been forming died in his throat. "What?" he stammered.

"You clearly don't care if she lives or dies, or you wouldn't be doing what you're doing."

"What am I doing?"

"Everyone knows you're making bipartisan overtures to the President. But you haven't made a statement. You haven't been explicit. You need to go on TV and come out in favor of the veterans aid bill."

Speaker Blaine was horrified. "I can't do that."

"Oh, I think you can," Abdul-Hakim said. And the line went dead.

The congressman stared at the phone in horror. What had he done? He hadn't demanded proof of life, and he'd refused their demands. And there was no way to reach them, to make things better, to straighten this out. Even if he did what they demanded, went on TV, created a political firestorm, it would take time, and they wouldn't know he was going to do it.

What would they do to his daughter?

39

Karen Blaine lay on the mattress in the tiny cabin and tried to free herself. In the locked room they hadn't bothered to tie her, because they thought she couldn't escape. Here, they kept her tied all the time.

The knot on the rope around her wrists wasn't a good knot. She knew that from summer camp. Not that she'd tried to tie knots in camp, but that dweeb Ralphie did, the one all the kids knew was a loser. When Ralphie tried to tie a square knot he would tie a weak granny knot, which was like a square knot only it would come undone. And that's the type of knot this was. She figured the big man must have tied it.

Karen fumbled with the knot, but it was hard working behind her back. With her wrists tied she could barely reach the rope, and she could only use one hand at a time.

What saved her was her fingernails. Her nails were backed by acrylics, a luxury she'd pampered herself with after breaking up with her boyfriend. It hadn't made her feel better, but it was helping her now. She'd used her reinforced nails to get a purchase on the rope, and the badly tied knot was finally loosening. There was suddenly room between her wrists. Before she knew it she was slipping her hands out, rubbing her wrists to restore the circulation.

She drew her legs up to where she could reach the ropes around her ankles. She had them off in a minute. She placed them quietly on the mattress, sat up, looked around.

The Arab came in the door.

Karen flinched, expecting punishment, but he didn't seem concerned. "Ah, you're up. Good. We won't have to untie you."

The Arab was carrying the black satchel. He set it on the floor, stooped, and took something out. His back was to her, so she couldn't tell what it was.

He stood and turned, and she gasped.

He had a scalpel!

And in horror Karen suddenly realized why they had brought her here to this remote spot.

No one would be able to hear her scream.

40

Ann Keaton was hassled. It was tricky enough just being chief of staff. Being chief of staff during a national emergency was murder. Everybody wanted something. The speechwriters wanted to know what to say and the press secretary wanted to know what *not* to say and everybody else wanted to know what was happening, whether they needed to or not.

Sorting them out was her job, and no one was going to thank her for it. Oh, Kate would in the long run, but in the short term no one would appreciate what she was doing and everyone would blame her for what she wasn't.

Yesterday had been bad, and things hadn't eased up much today. It had been a tough morning. For the most part she'd managed to make Kate's secretary field requests for appointments with the President, but even so, Ann's nerves were frazzled. When she finally got a moment's respite, she groaned as her secretary opened the door.

Ann smiled when she saw who was being ushered in, however.

Paul Wagner was indeed a handsome man. Late forties, wavy black hair slightly flecked with gray, decked out like a fashion model in a stylish blue suit, Paul only had to smile to make Ann's troubles fade away.

Ann twined her arms around his neck. "What a pleasant surprise! I'm glad it's you and not someone else who wants something."

He kissed her, said, "I only want to take you to dinner."

Ann laughed. "You sure picked a great day."

"You canceled our last dinner."

"I know, I'm sorry about that — I'd much rather have dined with you than the congressman. And with everything that's been going on . . . well, it's been crazy around here."

"Any news about the shooting?"

"Not you, too."

Paul put up his hand and smiled. "Sorry. It's just everyone's talking about it. Of course you don't want to. It's your job. I'm here to take you away from all that. Have dinner with me. I promise we won't talk about anything job-related."

"That sounds wonderful. I wish I could."

The phone on Ann's desk rang. She looked at it in annoyance, disengaged herself from Paul's clutches, and picked it up. She listened, heaved a heavy sigh, said, "Yes, I'll take it." She pressed the flashing button on her phone, said, "I am sorry, Mr. Ambassador . . . Yes, these are distressing times."

Ann removed the phone from her ear, rolled her eyes, mimed jabber, jabber, jabber with her free hand, and mouthed, "Ask me tomorrow."

Paul nodded, blew her a kiss, and went out.

Paul hadn't expected Ann would be able to go out to dinner. He hadn't expected she'd tell him anything, either. Ann was a smart, savvy, independent woman, and part of what made her so good at her job was her unfailing self-command. In the months they'd been dating, Paul hadn't learned anything from Ann that he couldn't have seen on the evening news. Not that she didn't joke about her job, she did, but always with the utmost discretion.

Her secretary was another story. Julia was a born gossip, and quite susceptible to the charms of a handsome young man. Paul flirted with her shamelessly, to good advantage.

Julia was chatting on the phone, no doubt with one of the other White House secretaries, when Paul came out, but she hung up to flirt with him.

"So how'd it go this time?" Julia said.

Paul threw up his hands and grinned. "Shot down again!"

Julia laughed. "You just have no way with women."

"She claims she's busy." Paul perched jauntily on the edge of Julia's desk. "Should I believe her?"

"It's been crazy around here."

"Do tell."

Five minutes later Paul was out the door with a ton of information. Nothing vital, of course — even if she would mention state secrets, she didn't know any. But as far as everyday affairs were concerned, the woman was a major source.

Paul jerked his cell phone out of his pocket, but refrained from clicking it on. He had to make a call, but he wasn't going to do it from the White House. He was too familiar with the workings of the NSA to trust any communication within the walls or even on the grounds. It was only when he was safe on the streets of Washington that he made the call.

"It's me."

"I know who it is. Why are you calling?"

"The President's national security advisor called in a witness for questioning."

"Who?"

"A lawyer in the White House counsel's office."

"What lawyer?"

"A woman named Margo Sappington."

There was a pause. "Are you sure?"

"Yes. She had her in twice, yesterday and then again this morning."

"Why?"

"My source didn't know."

"Maybe you need a new source." Another pause. "Is that all you called for?"

"I thought you'd want to know."

"Do you have anything else?"

"No."

And the line went dead.

Paul stared at the phone. These guys certainly never massaged his ego. They ought to be damn grateful he was so good at what he did. He was practically ready to call them on it. Let them try to find someone else handsome enough, suave enough, and clever enough to romance the President's chief of staff and come up with valuable information. And then they act as if he were just delivering a pizza.

Paul nodded in agreement with himself.

They were just lucky they paid so well.

41

Margo closed up her office and headed home. She lived within walking distance of the White House, a nice perk once she got the job. Margo had no car and hated public transportation. The buses were too slow, the Metro never let you off close enough to where you were going. A leisurely twenty-minute walk took about the same time as it would to be jostled in rush-hour traffic on the train.

It happened fast. Margo was just starting over the viaduct near her apartment. The gray van appeared out of nowhere and cruised beside her, mirroring her speed.

The side door slid open. Two masked men dressed in black hopped out, and before Margo could scream, a hand slid over her mouth, an arm wrapped around her shoulders, and her body, still in a firm embrace, was flung unceremoniously into the back of the van.

Struggling to free herself, Margo twisted her head.

There was a third man in the van. His face was not masked, and Margo recognized him. It was the man with Arab features, the phony CIA agent who'd talked to her before.

Then Margo felt a prick in her shoulder and everything faded to black, just as the side door of the van slid shut.

42

Margo Sappington was late for work, a strange enough occurrence to merit concern. A bright young lawyer in the White House counsel's office, Margo Sappington was never late. The event was unusual enough to attract the attention of Susan Granger, the secretary on the office switchboard. By ten o'clock she was worried enough to call Margo at home. There was no answer.

Susan frowned. She thought for a moment, picked up the phone, and dialed Holly Barker. "Holly, it's Susan Granger, over in legal. Did you talk to Margo Sappington yesterday?"

In the national security advisor's office, Holly shot a look at Teddy and clicked the phone on speaker. "I spoke to Margo, why?"

"She didn't come in this morning. I wondered if you might have given her some assignment that would have kept her out of the office."

"No, I didn't. She probably just overslept."

"She's not answering her phone."

"Her cell phone?"

"That's right."

"She probably forgot to turn it on. I'm sure she'll be in any minute."

"Well, let me know if you hear anything."

"Will do."

Holly clicked the button off. "Do you think something happened to her?"

"Let's not speculate," Teddy said. "She didn't come in, so we're going to check it out. Where does she live?"

"Hang on. Let me see." Holly called up the internal directory and scrolled through addresses of White House employees. "Other side of the viaduct."

"Is that walking distance?"

"Yes."

Teddy looked over Holly's shoulder, memorized the address at a glance. "Okay, carry on as usual. I'll be back."

"Carry on as usual?"

"You might check in with the President. Isn't that your job?"

Holly shook her head, chuckled. "It almost seems incidental."

Teddy left the White House. He checked his gun from habit. Not that he'd need it.

No terrorist was holding Margo Sappington hostage in her apartment waiting for him to come in the door. It was a simple situation. Margo Sappington had either overslept or not.

Teddy stepped along briskly, doing the twenty-minute walk in fifteen. The downstairs door was locked. It was a laughable affair, would have taken your average burglar sixty seconds. Teddy had it open in five. He climbed the stairs to the third floor.

The upstairs lock was more formidable. With his tools he'd have had no problem. Without them was a little harder. He was also trying not to leave scratches on the lock. If it came to that, the police would get the wrong impression.

Margo's apartment was a small one-bedroom affair, but in an exclusive locale. When Teddy opened the door he saw it was tastefully appointed, the few furnishings antique but exquisitely maintained and clearly chosen to make the most of the limited space. But the atmosphere was tainted by the overwhelming odor of stale whiskey.

The liquor was in the bedroom. The open bottle lay tipped over in the bed. There was a half-filled tumbler on the nightstand. A plastic pill bottle lay on its side. The cap was off, and gel-capped pills had spilled out. Seconal from the look of them.

And from the look of her.

Margo Sappington lay on her back in bed. She was dressed for work, but clearly from the day before. Her clothes were rumpled. Her makeup was smeared, and her head lolled to one side. Her eyes were open and staring.

A pill lay near her head, as if she'd tried to put it in her mouth and missed. Another gel-capped pill was in her left hand.

A cop would have no problem labeling Margo a suicide. She'd be just what he expected to find.

There was no reason to stick around. There was nothing Teddy could do for Margo Sappington, and nothing Margo Sappington could do for him. She had told him all he needed to know just by being dead.

Careful as ever not to leave fingerprints, Teddy eased himself out of the apartment and closed the door. He went back down the stairs and walked back to the White House. It was time to waste another burner phone. He was running through them like water.

Teddy whipped out the phone, called 911. "I'd like to report a dead woman."

"Who is this?"

"She appears to have overdosed on whiskey and pills." Teddy gave them the address. "There's nothing to be done for her, but you better get her out of there because she's going to start to stink."

"Who is this?"

Teddy hung up the phone. On his way over the viaduct, he threw it in the river.

43

The phone rang and Congressman Blaine jumped. But it wasn't his cell phone. It was the front desk. Though Congressman Blaine's primary residence was in his home state of Ohio, he kept an apartment in D.C. for when Congress was in session.

He scooped it up. "Yes?"

"You have a package."

"Oh?"

"Just arrived by messenger. Do you want to come down and get it, or should I lock it up?"

"I'll come down."

It was a bubble-wrap envelope. He didn't inquire who'd brought it, or whether the doorman had to sign for it, or any of the things he'd normally ask. He took it upstairs and fumbled in his pocket for his keys. He had a moment of panic that he'd forgotten them, that he'd left them in the apartment and he'd have to suffer the humiliation of having to get the super to let him in. But no, his keys were there. He opened the door and let himself into his apartment.

The bubble-wrap envelope was sealed tight. It was the self-sealing type, and they usually held pretty well. He was in no mood to deal with it. He found a pair of scissors in a kitchen drawer and snipped the end of the envelope off.

He shook the contents out on the kitchen table and recoiled in horror.

It was a bloody fingertip.

44

A Secret Service agent picked Stone up at his hotel, smuggled him into the White House through a back entrance, and ushered him into the Oval Office.

Kate rose to meet him.

"What's happened?" Stone said.

"The Speaker was just here. I sent him home so I could talk to you alone, and because I couldn't take it anymore."

"What happened?"

"He got a phone call from the kidnappers."

"Did he demand proof of life?"

"He never got a chance. They cut him off, said he wasn't cooperating. They demanded he go on TV and declare his support of the veterans aid bill. He said he couldn't do that, and they hung up."

"Did they call back?"

"No." Kate picked up the bubble-wrap envelope. "This morning this came by messenger."

"What is it?"

"Take a look."

Stone took the envelope, slid the bloody fingertip out onto the table.

"It's got to be his daughter's," Kate said. "That was why they sent him the copy of her rap sheet. So he'd have her fingerprints to compare it against."

"Good God! The poor man. It's a wonder he's holding it together."

"I don't think he will for long."

"What's he going to do?"

"I don't know, but I think he's going on TV."

"Aw, hell."

"Yes. I figure that when the kidnappers get what they want, they'll kill the girl."

"Probably right."

"I'm hoping they wait until the bill's passed."

"When is that?"

"The vote takes place at the end of the week."

"So what do you want to do?"

"It's hard to say when I don't know what the score is." Kate pointed to the bubble-wrap envelope. "Can you handle this?"

Stone nodded. "I'll verify it's the girl."

"I'll try to calm the Speaker down. That

may not work. If someone hurt my child, I don't know what I'd do."

"When's he going on TV?"

"I think as soon as his nerves are steady enough, he's going to do it. I'll try to talk him out of it if he gives me a chance, but I don't think he will. Can you help me?"

Stone nodded. "Let me see what I can do."

45

Stone met Teddy in the bar. "You look rested," Stone said.

"I got some sleep. I shouldn't have. Margo Sappington? The lawyer who bugged your phone?"

"What about her?"

"She's dead."

"What?"

"Of an apparent suicide."

"Why do you say *apparent?*"

"Give me a break. Did that girl strike you as someone with suicidal tendencies?"

"Certainly not."

"She didn't strike me that way, either. But Holly and I talked to her, and the next thing you know she's gobbling barbiturates."

"That's not her."

"That may not fit her personality profile, but she's certainly dead."

"What do the police think?"

"I couldn't say. They should be getting

there about now."

"I'm not sure I understand."

"It's probably better that way."

"What about the photo on the news of the Middle Eastern suspect?"

"He's the shooter."

"Is that confirmed?"

"It is for me. He's traveling with a phony driver's license."

"Why didn't they release the name?"

"They don't have it."

"Do you?"

Teddy smiled.

"Shouldn't you tell airport security?"

"No need. They have his photo. He's on a no-fly watch list. He's not going anywhere. Putting out his name would only tell the kidnappers we know, and get an old friend of mine killed."

"Well, you know best," Stone said. "Listen. I've got news, and it's not good."

"Oh?"

Stone set the padded envelope on the table.

"What's this?"

"A bloody fingertip. It was delivered to the Speaker this morning. Probably his daughter's."

"Shit."

"Here's her rap sheet. You can compare

the print and make sure."

"It's hers. These guys don't bluff."

"The Speaker's a basket case. They're asking him to go on TV and denounce his own party. I think he's going to do it."

"And God knows what they'll ask him then." Teddy exhaled. "All right. This is a wake-up call. We've got to speed things along."

46

Millie pulled the back off the cell phone, popped in the microchip, and slid the back into place.

Teddy clicked the stopwatch. "Two-point-seven."

"I can do better."

"I'm sure you can. What about your lift?"

"You want me to pick your pocket?"

"I'm a bad subject to practice on."

"Why?"

"I tend to react."

"You won't if you don't feel anything."

"I will, and it will wreck your confidence. You'll have to try someone else."

Teddy was teaching Millie how to lift a cell phone and place a bug. He was pretty sure she could do it, just not to him.

"Tell me about your hacker friend."

"He's good."

"I'm sure he is. Is he trustworthy?"

"Absolutely."

"You don't sound sure."

"If I tell him not to talk, he won't talk."

"I don't have time to vet him. This is all on you."

"I understand. I lose my job if he can't cut it. Do you think I want that to happen?"

"We all lose a lot more than that. All right, I'm taking him at your word. Give him a call."

"That won't work."

"Why not?"

Holly Barker smiled. "Young people don't call anymore. They text each other."

"Okay, text him, then."

"That won't work, either," Millie said. "Some days he doesn't even look at his texts."

"This is the dependable guy you vouch for?"

"He's fine in the areas you want. But I'll have to go see him in person."

"Why?"

"He's a little . . . eccentric."

47

Kevin Cushman, screen handle Warp-lord924, was twenty-eight years old, lived with his mother, and dressed for success in pajama bottoms, T-shirts, and bare feet. He spent the day in front of an entire wall of computer screens, hardwired together in a virtual spiderweb of cables. But he was no pathetic loser. He pulled down six figures a year solving people's computer problems. A high six figures. He was able to work mostly from home, which allowed him time for more important computer activities.

When Millie came in Kevin was killing horrible poison-dripping scorpion-centaurs in some far-off galaxy. Millie waited patiently for one of them to get him. Finally a poisoned tooth sank into the hero's arm and Kevin's champion died in the dust.

Kevin looked over his shoulder, said petulantly, "Now see what you made me do?"

"Sorry," Millie said. She knew from experience any other response would be worse.

His dead hero was somehow reconstituting himself, but Kevin put the game on pause so he could swing around in his chair to confront her. "That's what you always say. And you know what *I* always say. Sorry does not take back the hit or extract the poison. I can't power up until Level Twelve. I can only reboot at half-charge."

"Yeah, yeah, I know," Millie said. "Listen, Kevin, I have a job for you."

"I've got all the jobs I need."

"Yeah, well, you *want* this job."

"Huh?"

"This is a covert op. It's classified, something big. They need a man of your talents. You'll get clearance."

"That is way cool. What's the catch?"

"There's no catch."

"Come on, there's always a catch."

Millie considered. "Well, sort of."

"What?"

"You'll have to get dressed."

Kevin looked decidedly uncomfortable in a jacket and tie when Millie presented him to Holly Barker forty-five minutes later.

"Here he is," Millie said. "Holly, this is Kevin, aka Warplord924. Kevin, this is

Holly Barker."

Holly didn't get up. "Hi, Kevin. Do you know who I am?"

"I googled you."

"Of course. Then you realize anything you may hear will be highly classified."

"Does this have anything to do with the assassination?"

Holly ignored the question. "Here's the deal. You're on the team. You'll have highest priority clearance. Except for one thing."

"What's that?"

"There *is* no team. This is a covert operation. So covert it doesn't exist."

Holly got up, opened the door to the adjoining office. "You can set up in here. You're going to be monitoring a wiretap."

"Is it legal?"

"Very good question. Try to forget you asked it."

Kevin blinked.

Teddy, who'd been sitting unobtrusively off to the side, got to his feet. "Don't worry about it, Kevin. We're the good guys. We take care of our own." He walked Kevin into the next room where a swivel chair commanded a wall of computer equipment. "You monitor the tap from here. When a call comes in, trace it, and tell me where it came from."

"I'm not sure I can do that."

"Sure you can. Millie says you're the best."

In the other room Holly said, "Shit!"

"What's the matter?"

"He's on TV."

Teddy clapped his hands together. "Show-time."

48

Congressman Blaine pushed his way through the throng of TV reporters shouting questions and pointing microphones. He had just given a speech on the steps of Capitol Hill, stressing that now was not the time for party politics, now was the time for bipartisan unity, and urging Congress to act responsibly. He had stopped just short of asking Republicans to vote for the clean veterans aid bill, but the message was clear. Everyone knew what he meant.

It was a bombshell.

"Mr. Speaker! Mr. Speaker!" the TV reporters shouted.

He might not have heard them. He elbowed his way through them, gently at first, then more assertively. He should have had aides clearing the way for him, but he hadn't made any preparations, hadn't told anybody what he was doing. He had just shown up on the top steps of Capitol Hill and started speaking. And within minutes he had every camera in the vicinity aimed at him, with more members of the media arriving every minute.

It was a politician's dream, the type of publicity impossible to generate, except in this fashion, by committing political suicide.

Congressman Blaine walked down the steps on automatic pilot. He'd held himself together for the TV cameras, but as he plowed his way through the crowd, he was on the brink of tears. Still he held them back, his public persona hardwired into his system.

He had just cleared the crowd when his cell phone rang. He nearly jumped out of his skin. The phone was set very loud to make sure he heard it. He fished it out of his jacket pocket. "Hello?"

There was no one there.

He said, "Hello?" again, feeling like a fool, but terrified he might hang up on the kidnappers.

Finally he gave up and stuck the phone back in his pocket.

He turned a corner, ran into the girl, and knocked her down. He'd been preoccupied with the phone, hadn't realized she was there. Muttering apologies, he stooped to help her up.

Millie missed the grab. She knew where the phone was from watching him answer her call, and she'd done the pickpocket's move perfectly, bumping him in the stomach so he wouldn't feel the hand in his jacket pocket, but the phone slipped through her fingers. The poor man was sweating from his ordeal, and the phone was wet from his perspiration.

She had to go double-dipping, a no-no in the trade. The danger escalates exponentially on the second try. A pro would leave the mark and find fresh game. Millie didn't have that option. She slipped and fell into him, got her hand inside his jacket, tugged the cell phone out.

It wasn't the perfect move. He grabbed for his lapel as if he'd felt his jacket ripping. He had to let go of Millie to do it, and she slid to the ground, curling her hands underneath her and landing on her forearms.

She flicked the back off the cell phone, held it between two fingers, and grabbed the chip she'd been palming with her forefinger and her thumb. In her head she counted the seconds as she clicked the chip in place and slid the back on.

She came to her feet, apologizing for bumping into him, thanking him for helping her up, and straightening his jacket, a

212

perfectly natural thing to do since she'd certainly mussed his clothing.

Moments later she was hurrying off to whatever important appointment she'd been preoccupied with when she bumped into him.

As soon as she was out of sight, Millie whipped out her own cell phone and called Kevin.

"Target is live."

49

The reaction was fast and furious. Speaker Blaine had barely gotten home before Congressman Herman Foster was on CNN disclaiming everything that the Speaker had said. "Speaker Blaine does not speak for the Republican Party when he advocates betraying the trust of our constituents by abandoning the principles on which we were elected."

Congressman Blaine went in the kitchen and poured himself a drink to calm his nerves. He went back to the living room, where Herman Foster had been replaced on CNN by Congressman Sam Snyder, presenting the opposing viewpoint.

His cell phone rang. He had left it on the coffee table, didn't trust it in his pocket. He snatched it up.

"Yes?" he said breathlessly.

"What the hell are you doing? Have you lost your mind?"

It took Congressman Blaine a moment to place the voice. When he did, his heart nearly stopped. Calvin Hancock! The last person in the world he wanted to talk to now.

Calvin Hancock was not a man you could brush off. He had spent over a million dollars on the Speaker's campaign. The situation did not matter. When Calvin Hancock called, you answered.

"Sir —"

"Have you forgotten who your friends are? Have you forgotten who funded your campaign?"

"No, sir, I —"

"Your fellow Republicans seem to think so. Or haven't you noticed."

"You mean Herman Foster?"

"Is anyone else calling you out on national TV? I'm sure they will. He's just the first."

"I'll call Herman. We have a relationship."

"Not anymore, you don't. Weren't you watching? The gentleman made his feelings pretty clear."

"I know, sir, and —"

"If that's not bad enough, I've got to watch that idiot Sam Snyder *supporting* you on national television. Sam fucking Snyder, who's not only the opposition, he's a personal family friend of the President. *Prais-*

215

ing you on TV."

The phone bleeped.

Speaker Blaine jumped. He pulled it from his ear, looked at it.

Caller Unknown.

That was them!

That was the call!

"I have another call," he said helplessly.

"More important than mine?"

"No, sir, of course not. But —" His mind whirled, searching for a reason. He couldn't find one. "I have to take it," he said, and broke the connection. He'd pay for that later. He didn't care. He clicked on the new call.

It was the voice he'd come to dread. "You didn't do what we asked."

"I did. Weren't you watching?"

"I was. You were supposed to tell Republicans to vote for the bill."

"I said we need a bipartisan effort."

"Did I ask you to give them a *hint*? Go back on TV and tell them *directly* to vote for the bill."

"I can't do that."

"You'll do what we say or your daughter dies."

He steeled himself. "Let me talk to her."

"That's not going to happen."

"Why not?"

"Because I'm not going to let you."

"How do I know she's alive?"

"She's alive."

"How do I know?"

"I told you."

"Why should I believe you?"

"You have no choice."

"I don't care. I can't go on not knowing. I have to know she's alive. If you can't prove she's alive, then she must be dead." His voice broke. "Is she dead? Is my daughter dead? If she's dead you get nothing, you understand, nothing. I've done everything you asked. You have no reason to hurt her."

"Don't give me a reason."

"I'm not, I'm not! I'm telling you to keep her alive! You get nothing unless you keep her alive. Prove it to me. Prove it to me or you get nothing. Do you hear me? Nothing."

The phone clicked dead.

50

Kevin ripped off his headset. "Jesus Christ!"

"Where's the call from?" Teddy said.

"They're going to kill her!"

"Snap out of it. Trace the call."

"It wasn't long enough to get an exact location."

"You got something."

"It was a cell phone here in D.C. I can probably pinpoint it within a twenty-block radius, but that's the best I can do. He has to keep them on the line longer."

"We don't have control over that. He doesn't know we're doing this, so we have to work with what we've got. Now then, you've got a cell phone in a twenty-block radius. What else have you got?"

"Nothing. It's a throwaway phone, and it isn't registered. There's no way to trace the owner, just the location. If they call back I can pin it down, but with a throwaway phone, they probably won't."

"What about the other call? What can you tell about that?"

"That one was different. It came from a landline, which will be listed. Hang on, I'll trace it." He typed rapidly. "Got it. The phone's listed in the name of Calvin Hancock."

Holly Barker sucked in her breath.

Kevin looked at her. "What?"

"Big money man," Teddy said. "All right, that tears it. As if the Speaker wasn't under enough pressure. Once Calvin Hancock gets involved, the situation's out of control. He spends a ton of money and he expects results."

"Any way to stop him?" Millie said.

"Short of killing him, no. He won't be put off and he won't be distracted. It couldn't have come at a worse time. Just when the Speaker got the nerve to stand up to these guys."

Teddy's cell phone rang. He fished it out of his pocket. "Hello?"

"Mr. Worthing?"

It took Teddy a second to place the name. It was the one he'd used to rent the hangar at Dulles where he'd left Peter's plane. "Yes. One moment please." He covered the phone. "I have to take this. Millie, stay with Kevin. Keep on top of the Speaker's calls.

He should be getting a lot."

Teddy followed Holly into her office, shut the door, and uncovered the phone. "This is Mr. Worthing. What's up?"

"I had some men snooping around the hangar checking out your plane. They seemed particularly interested in the tail numbers."

"Oh, yeah?"

"Yeah. The decal of one of the numbers was peeling up on the corner. The guy tried to pull it off. I stopped him. But they had a lot of questions."

"What did you tell them?"

"I told them to take a hike. If they weren't from Federal Aviation they got no right to ask."

"And these guys weren't?"

"Just goons. They didn't even bother to flash credentials."

"Did they leave peacefully?"

"They asked a lot more questions. I didn't answer them."

"What did they want to know?"

"When was the hangar rented, how long was it rented for?"

"What did you tell them?"

"I told them they were wasting their time, the hangar wasn't available, but there were plenty more to rent right next door."

"Did that satisfy them?"

"Hell no. They wanted to know about Billy Barnett. They seemed to think he was the pilot."

"Thanks. They got no right to be there. Let me know if they come back."

Teddy hung up.

"What was that?" Holly said.

"They just found Peter's plane. They had a bug in Stone's phone when he called me to come out here and told me to borrow it. They tried to take me out at the airport. When the item 'Movie Producer Billy Barnett Shot Dead' didn't show up in the tabloid press, they started tracing the plane. I changed the tail numbers, but they found it anyway."

"How bad is that?"

"Well, it isn't good. Now they know Billy Barnett's in D.C. They suspected it before, but this confirms it."

"But they don't know who Billy Barnett is."

"No. As far as they're concerned, he's just a movie producer from L.A. But the harder he is to pin down, the more interested they'll become. They can't kill him, and they can't find him. The plane they think he's flying has the tail numbers changed. They keep coming up empty. It will drive them nuts. They'll become obsessed with Billy Barnett."

"So what are you going to do?"

"Let them find him."

51

Teddy Fay called the concierge and asked to have valet service bring around his car. He'd rented both the car and his hotel room on Billy Barnett's credit card. He'd changed into his Billy Barnett guise to match the ID photo on his driver's license.

He spotted the two men right away. They were small-time thugs, and they probably weren't used to following anyone who was familiar with surveillance techniques, because they weren't very good at it. One was pretending to be waiting for someone, and he oversold it by looking at his watch every fifteen seconds. The other was reading a newspaper. He wasn't holding it upside down, but he might as well have been for all the attention he was paying to it. As if that weren't bad enough, they gave each other the high sign when he walked out, and they climbed into a gold Oldsmobile way too flashy for the job. Teddy led them through a few turns just to make sure, but he needn't have bothered. It was obvious who they were.

And what they wanted.

Teddy drove to a downtown mall and pulled into a parking garage. He drove up to level 5, which wasn't crowded, and parked. He locked his car and headed for the elevator.

The gold Oldsmobile pulled up next to his car. Two men got out and followed him. They picked up the pace and closed the gap.

A gunshot stopped them in their tracks. It came from the direction of their car. They spun around, crouching and starting to reach for their guns.

There was no one there.

They turned back.

There was no one there, either.

The man they were following was gone.

They looked at each other, baffled.

Teddy Fay stepped up behind them and shoved guns in their backs.

"Let's hold it right there," Teddy said. "What you feel is the silencer of a gun. If you're wondering why your partner doesn't make a move, I have a gun on him, too. So, let's put your hands on your heads and walk back to the golden Olds."

Teddy marched them back to their car.

"All right, turn around slow." Teddy waggled his gun on the big thug. "You, with your left hand, reach in your buddy's jacket, take out his gun with two fingers, and put it on the ground. That's right." He motioned to the now-disarmed man. "Now you do the same to him. Good. Now step back."

They did.

Teddy pointed to a black spot on the ground next to his car. "The shot you heard was a firecracker. Remarkably cheap and effective. Illegal, I'm afraid, but you can't have everything."

Teddy studied his assailants' faces as he picked up their guns. They were clearly nothing special, just your run-of-the-mill thugs. The big one had a crew cut and his face was scarred, like a prizefighter who'd hung around a bit too long. The smaller one looked street-smart, with animal cunning.

"Nothing to be worried about," Teddy said. "We're just going to have a little talk. First of all, who's in charge?"

The small thug's eyes flicked toward his buddy.

Teddy shot the small thug in the face. He crumpled to the pavement.

"Funny," Teddy said, "I would have thought it was him. So, you're the brains of the outfit. If you want to survive this meeting, you're going to tell me everything you know."

The big thug gawked at him. His lip quivered.

"You got the car keys?"

"Yeah."

"Pop the trunk."

The thug took out his car keys, pushed a button, and zapped the trunk open.

Teddy gestured with his gun. "Put him in."

The thug hefted his dead buddy to his feet, propped his stomach over the edge of the trunk, and flipped him in.

Teddy gestured with the gun. "You too."

The thug looked alarmed. He clearly expected to be shot. He climbed in with a sense of resignation.

"Give me the keys."

The thug handed them over.

Teddy slammed the trunk. He popped the trunk of his rental car and took the bolt cutters he'd requisitioned from the CIA out of his gear bag. He threw them on the floor of the thug's car, hopped in, and drove down the exit ramps, level by level, and out of the garage.

One of Teddy's favorite places, back when D.C. was his stomping grounds, was an abandoned boat ramp just fifteen miles out of town. *Boat ramp* was perhaps a flattering description for the overgrown dirt road sloping down to the river. Teddy had made use of it often in his stint with the CIA. He hoped it was still there.

It was. A simple turn off the highway, unmarked except for the two weathered wooden posts holding up the chain across the road. The chain itself was invisible in the overgrowth. Teddy stopped short of it and got out of the car. The chain was held in place with a heavy-duty padlock, and Teddy didn't want to waste time on it with a live thug in his trunk. He took out the bolt cutters and snapped the chain.

Teddy drove over the chain, pulled in, maneuvered a U-turn, and backed up to the riverbank. He got out, popped the trunk.

The thug poked his head out, blinked in the sunlight, and found himself looking at a gun.

"Have a nice ride?" Teddy said. "Get out."

The thug climbed out of the trunk.

"Okay, let's you and me have a little talk. I'm going to ask you some questions. Each time you get one wrong, I'm going to shoot you somewhere. Sooner or later, I'll hit something you need. Ready? Let's begin. Who hired you?"

"I don't know."

227

Teddy shot him in the foot. "Wrong answer."

The thug cried out and doubled up in pain.

"You might want to think about your answers a little. You don't want to just blurt out the first thing that comes to mind, because your default setting is to lie. As you can see, lying will do you no good. Let's try again. Who hired you?"

"A guy in a bar."

"What guy?"

"Guy I never seen before. He comes up to me in this bar I hang out in. Joey's Place."

"Not exactly your high-end establishment."

"It's a dive, but drinks are cheap. Guy said he was told to look me up."

"Did he give you his name?"

"No."

"What did he look like?"

"Egyptian, Arab, whatever. I can never tell those guys apart."

"Did he have a hat? A beard? Long hair? How was he dressed?"

"No hat. No beard. Short hair. Suit and tie. Could have been a business executive. But he wasn't American, you know what I mean?"

Teddy showed him the photo of the man

with the SUV. "Is this the guy?"

The thug peered closely at the photo. "You know, it could be. He asked me if I wanted a job."

"What was the job?"

"Take someone out."

"Who?"

The thug grimaced. "Billy Barnett."

Teddy nodded. "How were you supposed to find him?"

"Hotel reservations."

"And airplane hangar rentals?"

"That's right. He said they might not be under that name. But the plane was a Cessna. He gave me the tail numbers."

"How do you contact this guy? Tell him it's done?"

"He said don't bother, he'll know."

"That's kind of scary."

"No kidding."

"But you must have some way to reach him. Some number you could call."

"No. He didn't want to see me again."

"How were you going to get paid?"

"He paid me in advance."

"In cash?"

"Yeah."

Teddy held out his hand. The thug made a face.

"You're not going to earn it," Teddy said.

"Why should you have it? Hand it over."

The thug pulled a wad of money out of his jacket pocket, reluctantly held it out.

Teddy stuck it in his pocket. "You paid your buddy yet?"

"No."

"Then we don't need him. Get him out of there."

"You want me to dump him in the river?"

"You got a problem with that?"

The thug put his hands under his buddy's armpits, lifted him up, and hefted his body out of the trunk. He wrestled him down to the river and flopped him in.

The dead man floated on his stomach. His feet caught in the reeds. The thug bent over, grabbed his ankles, freed the body, and gave it a push.

Teddy shot him in the head. The thug pitched into the water face-first. The two bodies floated away from shore.

Teddy slammed the trunk, got back in the car, and drove out the dirt road. As he turned onto the highway he made a mental note to call up and report the broken chain. Someone needed to get that fixed. After all, they wouldn't want just any old riffraff using the boat ramp.

52

Abdul-Hakim's two hit men were found floating facedown in the Potomac.

Calvin Hancock did not take the news well. "Two men couldn't handle him?"

"He must have got the drop on them."

"He wasn't following them, they were following him."

"There must be more to this Billy Barnett than we know."

"That's obvious. What are you doing about it?"

"Right now we're trying to find him."

"You lost him again?"

"He checked out of his hotel. We're watching for activity on his credit card, but so far there's been none."

"What about his plane?"

"It's still in the hangar. If he picks it up, we'll know."

"If he picks it up, it will be very good news. I can't wait for him to go back to

California. Which is not a bad idea. If you can't find him, send him home."

"How?"

"Kill his wife."

53

Shooting was going well. Ben had managed to take time off from running the studio to fill in for Teddy as producer. The transition was seamless. Ben had been Peter's producer before taking over the studio, so it wasn't like he had to learn the job. He just walked on the set and everything fell into place.

Betsy was strangely ambivalent. She liked Ben, and she wanted shooting to go well. She just didn't want it to go well without Teddy. More to the point, she wanted it to go better when Teddy was there. All day long she couldn't help watching the filming, seeing the scenes ticked off the schedule, and thinking Teddy would have done it more smoothly.

To her surprise, it wasn't bad working with Mike Freeman's men. The first day on the set she was aware of their presence. By the next day they had faded into the scenery.

She could not have picked them out from the cadre of extras waiting to be chosen as background action. The only time they made their presence felt was during the drive home.

Home, for the time being, was still Peter's house. Betsy'd been back to her house, but only in the company of one of Mike Freeman's men, and only to inspect the job the cleanup crew she'd hired had done with the damage.

Peter and Hattie were good hosts. For newlyweds, they could not have been more accommodating. After day shoots Betsy could have cocktails on the veranda, or lounge by the pool. She could take an outdoor shower on her own private terrace, watch TV in the sitting room of her suite, prepare any snack she wanted in Peter's well-stocked kitchen.

The only problem she had was falling asleep. She'd grown used to having Teddy in her bed, and without his comforting presence nothing seemed quite right. Which, of course, it wasn't. Teddy was a million miles away in the middle of a crisis, and the only information she was getting was messages relayed through Stone Barrington and his son. There were huge gaps in the narration, and she could imagine what things she wasn't being told.

Today she'd heard only that there'd been trouble and Teddy had "handled the situation." This did not cheer her. Knowing Teddy, "handled the situation" took in a lot of territory.

Betsy couldn't calm down. She tried watching the news channels, but there was no news, just a rehash of everything she'd already seen. She tried a sitcom, a talk show, an HBO movie. Nothing helped.

She finally switched the TV off and lay there in the dark, but it was a long time before she got to sleep.

The two men broke in at two in the morning. The smart one, Vinnie, stripped the wire and installed the bypass so he could cut the alarm without sending every cop in Beverly Hills rushing to the address before they could even open the door. He walked quietly across the patio and prayed that numbnuts Pug would do the same.

Vinnie whipped out a glass cutter and sliced a six-inch square in one of the panes of the door. He tapped gently all around the cut, then harder in one corner. The square broke away, the corner he tapped swiveled in, the opposite corner swiveled out. He grabbed the square, extracted it carefully, and tossed it gently onto a padded lounge chair. He reached his arm through, had a moment of panic he wouldn't be able to reach the lock. That asshole Pug would never let him forget it. His fingers touched the doorknob and the lock snapped open.

Vinnie looked meaningfully at Pug, raised a warning finger to his lips. Moments later they were inside. No alarm went off, no lights came on. Vinnie held up his hand to stop Pug, and they listened for the sound of movement. Nothing.

"Which way?" Pug whispered, much too loudly.

Vinnie rolled his eyes, and made a mental note never to work with Pug again. He'd been making that same resolution for years.

Vinnie jammed his finger to his lips, motioning for Pug to follow. He turned and tiptoed across the room.

To the right was the hallway down to the bedrooms. To the left, the archway to the living room, dining room, and kitchen.

A door clicked open.

Vinnie wheeled around, grabbed Pug, pulled him into the shadows.

There was a dim light coming from the end of the hallway to the right. Then the sound of footsteps, bare feet padding along the hall.

Betsy Barnett came out in a nightgown, made her way through the semidarkness across the central hallway and through the doorway to the kitchen. She crossed the kitchen in the dark. She was pretty sure the kitchen light couldn't be seen from Peter and Hattie's room, still she didn't want to take the chance of waking them. She maneuvered around the center island, groped her way toward the refrigerator.

Betsy heard something. She stopped. Listened. Heard nothing. She'd been under a lot of stress the past few days. She was probably just jumpy.

Pug sucked in his breath and held it, an automatic reaction since Vinnie had recently started razzing him about snorting like a wild boar. He stood there, frozen like a statue, not ten feet from Betsy Barnett, his right hand curled around the knife. He couldn't see Betsy in the dark, but he knew she was there.

Betsy couldn't see Pug, either. She'd heard the sharp intake of breath, didn't know what it was. Now she heard nothing, saw nothing.

She must have imagined it.

Betsy reached for the refrigerator, found the door handle, pulled it open.

Pug's first thought was, how can a small appliance bulb be so bright? Before he realized that *all* the lights were on, strong arms grabbed him from behind, wrestled him sideways, and slammed his head down on the butcher block top of the center island.

When Pug was jerked upright again his hands were handcuffed behind him, the woman he'd been following was gone, and Vinnie, also handcuffed, was being hauled into the kitchen by two men.

A man stood in the center of the kitchen. He was smiling, but his face was hard.

"Well, gentlemen," Mike Freeman said, "it's going to be a while before the police get here. I've got a few questions."

54

Teddy insisted on speaking to Mike Freeman himself. He didn't like risking it, but
he had to get the news firsthand.

"You're sure they were after her?"

"Absolutely. She was the target."

"Was it a hit or a snatch?"

"That's the only bone of contention. They
say it was a snatch job only, but they would.
Given a choice, you don't cop to attempted
murder. Even the big dumb one knew that,
and he didn't know much. He was caught
sneaking up on her with a knife in his hand,
so that story isn't going to wash."

"How'd he explain that?"

"Not very well. Thinking fast is not his
strong suit. He couldn't come up with any
useful euphemism. Even the phrase *knock
her out* escaped him. The guy's a paid assassin, but how he made it this far without
anyone cleaning his clock escapes me.

"The other guy's something else. Lives by

his wits, street-smart, can't be happy he was saddled with the goon. I assume it wasn't his choice."

"Whose choice was it?"

"That's where it gets interesting. The street-smart guy won't talk without a deal on the table. The big goon is too dumb to cut a deal. He's the type who gets bored and nods out halfway through the Miranda warning. He told us a lot, I just wish he knew more."

"What did he know?"

"They work for a small-time boss named Carlo Gigante. He gave them the orders to snatch Betsy Barnett. What they were supposed to do once they had her gets hazy, probably because it wasn't a snatch to begin with. There's every indication they were going to kill her to send a message."

"So the goon rolled on Gigante?"

"That's right."

"Then he's in trouble."

"Same with the other guy, though he didn't talk. As long as Gigante thinks they did, they can't be long for this world."

"And all they know is they were hired by Gigante?"

"Right."

"Did the police pick him up?"

"Yeah, for all the good it did."

"What's he say?"

"He won't talk, but his lawyer's talking plenty. Gigante doesn't know them, they don't know him, they're mistaken, they're lying, the real guy who hired them paid them to tell this story, he has no idea what they're talking about, this is a shakedown, this is a case of false arrest."

"That's all?"

"The lawyer just got the case. Give him time. Anyway, we can't get anything out of Gigante."

"It doesn't matter. He'll have been hired by a voice on the phone."

"Yeah. Look, I know you want to come out here, but there's nothing you can do. Betsy's fine. My guys are good, and I'm on the scene myself. I don't know what you're faced with, but it looks like Stone needs you more than I do. Do you need backup?"

"It would just complicate things. I've got enough problems dodging the CIA."

"My men wouldn't get underfoot."

"Your men couldn't turn around without tripping over an agent. There's been an assassination, in case you hadn't heard."

"All right. Well, don't worry about us. I'm out here, I'm on top of it, we're fine. Just holler if you need anything."

Teddy hung up. He should have felt reassured, but he didn't. Mike was a good man.

But he was better.

55

Teddy Fay and Stone Barrington picked up Peter's jet at the airport. The pilot helped them roll it out of the hangar.

"Those men haven't been back, Mr. Worthing," the pilot said.

"I doubt if they will," Teddy said. "I think you scared them off."

"Mr. Worthing?" Stone grinned as they climbed into the cockpit.

"I didn't want to put it in Peter's name, and I wasn't going to put it in mine."

"No kidding."

Teddy took off and flew to Teterboro, where they swapped the Cessna for Stone's Citation. Stone flew and Teddy caught the first good sleep he'd had in a long time.

Mike Freeman was waiting when they set down in Santa Monica.

"Nice ride," Mike said. "I see you traded up."

"It's mine," Stone said.

"No kidding. I told you I could handle this."

"I'm sure you can," Teddy said. "But I take it personally when someone tries to kill my wife."

"I understand. I didn't think you had the time."

"It helps to have a private jet," Teddy said. "Don't take this as a knock on your competence, Mike. I just need to do things you wouldn't do."

"You're going to kill Gigante?"

"Do you really want to know?"

"Hell, no."

"Where is he?"

Mike pulled out his cell phone. "Let me check."

Teddy's face darkened. "You haven't lost him?"

"Don't be silly. I'm checking his exact location as of now." Mike punched in a number. "Yeah? . . . Still there? . . . Same situation? . . . Fine." He hung up. "He's at the Palm Palace, a nightclub outside L.A. He's in the company of a 'young lady,' and I'm getting that in quotes, so she might be hired. He's also in the company of a couple of goons."

"Not the ones who broke in?"

"Not a chance. They gave Gigante up,

they're persona non grata. They're lucky they're not floating in the bay."

"How far is it?"

"Half hour to forty-five minutes, depending on traffic. Do you want backup?"

"No. I'm going in alone."

"You're the boss."

Teddy pointed at Stone. "He's the boss. I'm the fussy client."

The car Mike provided was a black Chevy sedan. Teddy popped the trunk and slung his bag of equipment in. He opened it up, pushed aside the sniper's rifle, and selected the handgun with the silencer he'd designed himself. Teddy unscrewed the silencer from the gun, slipped them into his jacket pockets.

"What's the address of the nightclub?"

"It's already in the GPS."

"How do I switch it on?"

"Just start the engine."

Teddy got in and started the car. The screen on the dashboard lit up with the destination.

"Are you sure you don't want me to come along?" Mike said.

"To keep me out of trouble? Wouldn't work, and then *you'd* be *in* trouble. No, hang out with Stone. Catch up on old times. Where does Peter think you are?"

Mike Freeman smiled. "He never knows I'm there, he won't know I'm gone."

"Perfect. See you soon."

Teddy pulled out and sped away.

56

Traffic was light, and Teddy made the drive in under half an hour.

The nightclub was lit up in neon, a gaudy affair. The parking lot was nearly full. Teddy drove around and found a spot as close to the door as possible. He took the gun and silencer out of his pocket, put them in the glove compartment, and locked the car.

A beefy bouncer was keeping out objectionables, but in a suit and tie, Teddy breezed right by.

The nightclub was the size of a football field. On the stage a girl singer was crooning to a ten-piece band. The tempo was insistent and the volume was high. She wasn't half bad, but no one was listening.

It wasn't hard to spot the VIP tables. They had plush semicircular couches facing the stage for the high and mighty with chairs for the lesser in their party.

Carlo Gigante sat on one of the couches.

He was plump but solid, with a hard face. A scar down the side of his chin completed the image. He was smoking a cigar, and no one was telling him to put it out.

A young woman at least thirty years his junior was curled up on the couch with her head on his shoulder. Two bodyguards flanked them on the chairs. They were not as beefy as the bouncer, but probably twice as tough.

Teddy walked up to the table. The two bodyguards stood and stopped him.

"Mr. Gigante," Teddy said. "Call off your dogs. You and I need to have a little talk."

"You a cop?"

"No. This is just casual."

"Frisk him."

One of the goons patted Teddy down. "He's clean."

Gigante gestured with his cigar. "I don't like strangers who talk to me. Apparently, you don't know that. You need to learn. Take him out back and teach him."

The goons spun Teddy around and marched him toward the door. As they went out the bouncer said, "You need some help?"

"We're fine."

Instead of heading for the parking lot, the goons went around the building to the left.

Teddy had a feeling they'd done this before and knew exactly where they were going and exactly what they were doing. They just weren't very good at it. They were small-time hoods. Patting Teddy down for a weapon, they'd ignored little things like a handkerchief, change, a lighter, and a Chap-Stick. As they marched him into the shadows, Teddy managed to get a hand in his pocket and palm the ChapStick.

They went past the kitchen door, which was open, to the garbage dumpsters in the very back, his likely destination.

"Turn him around," the goon said.

The other guy grabbed Teddy's shoulders. The moment his arm was free, Teddy raised the ChapStick, which was really a small tube of Mace, and shot him in the eyes.

The goon screamed and let go of him. Teddy kicked him in the groin, spun around, and Maced the other goon flush in the face. He screamed and rubbed his eyes.

Teddy could have punched him, but there was no need to hurt his hand. A two-by-four was sticking out of the dumpster. Teddy grabbed it and brought it down hard on the goon's head. He went down like a rock.

The other goon was still holding his crotch. Teddy swung the two-by-four and put him out, too. He picked up their guns and dropped them in the dumpster, then he dragged the goons into the shadows, dusted off his clothes, and went back.

Teddy was somewhat disoriented coming from the direction of the kitchen, but he clicked the zapper until the headlights of his rental car flashed. He hopped in, opened the glove compartment, took out the hand-gun, and screwed the silencer on. He stuck it under his belt, and headed back into the nightclub.

The bouncer was surprised to see him.

"Those guys did need your help," Teddy said, jerking his thumb in that general direction.

The bouncer blinked uncomprehendingly and looked where he was pointing, while Teddy walked right by.

57

Teddy walked up to Carlo Gigante's table, sat down on the couch on the side that wasn't draped with a young woman, and stuck a gun in his ribs. "Your guys changed their minds. They decided we *should* have a little talk. Now, this gun has a silencer so I can shoot you three times and be out the door before anyone even notices anything is wrong. Or we can have a nice talk, and you can go back to entertaining your young lady. Your choice."

Gigante wet his lips. "What do you want to know?"

"This is a private talk. Tell your lady friend to go powder her nose. Tell her if she comes back with the bouncer or anyone at all, you will be very angry or dead."

Gigante said something to her in Italian. The young lady rolled her eyes, got up, and left.

"Excellent," Teddy said. "Here's the deal.

You sent two goons to kill a Hollywood producer's wife. They failed, and named you. I figure they're not the two who were here tonight, because the two who fingered you are either demoted or dead. I don't care about them. I don't care about you. I want to know who hired you."

"Go fuck yourself."

"See, now that's the wrong answer. If that's the answer, you're no use to me, and I shoot you and go ask someone else. Last chance. Who hired you? I'll give you three. One, two —"

Gigante put up his hand. "Hang on. Hang on. It's just a guy."

"I'm afraid that's not going to cut it."

"I know, I know. There's this guy. Sometimes he needs work done that he's not equipped to do."

"And you are?"

"What do you think?"

"What's this guy's name?"

"I don't know."

Teddy frowned. "Maybe you're no use to me after all."

"No, no," Gigante said quickly. "I never met him. He's a voice on the phone."

"Do you expect me to believe that?"

"It's true."

"What does he sound like, this voice on

the phone?"

"What do you mean?"

"Stop stalling for time and give me everything you've got. Did he have a high voice or a low voice? Did he talk fast or slow? Was he aggressive or pleasant? Did he have an accent?"

"He had an accent."

"What kind of accent?"

"I don't know. Arab. Afghan. Something Middle Eastern."

"So that's how it is, is it?"

"Don't get the wrong idea. He's not like that."

"Like what?"

"You know, political. He's not a terrorist."

"I see. He's like you."

Gigante opened his mouth, and closed it again.

"Why would you trust a foreign voice on the phone?"

"His money's good, and he pays in advance."

"You give him a refund on the producer's wife?"

"I'll get around to it."

"Did he ask for it back?"

"No."

"Why not?"

Gigante shrugged.

"Let's call him and ask him. Or you can simply refuse, and I'll find him on my own. Your call."

Teddy didn't say what would happen if he refused. He didn't have to.

Gigante reached in his pocket and took out a cell phone.

Teddy put up his hand. "No, no. Not that phone. Put it on the table. That's the type of phone you press a panic button and suddenly this table is surrounded with men. Use my phone."

Teddy pushed his cell phone across the table.

Gigante picked it up and punched in a number. "You know who this is? . . . Yeah. I got a man here wants to talk to you about the job that didn't happen. Talk to him, will you?" He handed the phone to Teddy.

"Hi, there," Teddy said. "Mr. Gigante has a problem because he took money from you and didn't deliver. I fix problems. I take care of them for Mr. Gigante, and I take care of them for you. So who do I owe? You, or the man you work for? You tell me, and I'll make it right."

The line went dead.

Teddy looked up from the phone. "He said it's Gigante's fault, kill him."

Gigante turned pale. Perspiration trickled

down the scar on his chin.

"But I'm not going to do that. You're off the hook for now. Whether you stay that way depends on whether anyone bothers me when I leave."

Teddy prodded Gigante with the silencer. "And whether you make another move on the producer's wife. If you do, I'll be back. And you don't want me back."

Teddy stood up, tucked his gun in his belt, and slipped his cell phone back in his pocket.

"Your boys should be waking up about now." Teddy chuckled and cocked his head. "If I were you, I wouldn't go anywhere without them."

Teddy came out of the nightclub and called Kevin. "Did you get the number?"

"Yeah, but it's no help. It was a burner phone somewhere in L.A. Right after they hung up they turned it off, probably trashed it. No way to trace it now."

"That's what I expected. But it was worth a shot."

Teddy hung up and called Stone. "We're done. Meet me at the airport."

There was no traffic on the freeway. Teddy made good time getting back.

Mike and Stone were waiting at the hangar.

"What's the story?" Stone said.

Teddy shook his head. "It's no-go."

"Gigante wouldn't crack?"

"Gigante gave him up, but the guy he gave me is a dead end."

"How come?"

"Gigante was hired by a Middle Eastern man somewhere in the Los Angeles area. For the time being, that's the best I can do. On the other hand, I doubt if Mr. Gigante is going to be bothering anyone in the near future. The gentleman is going to have his hands full."

Teddy popped the trunk, took out his bag of gear, and set it on the ground. He held out his hand to Mike Freeman. "Thank you, Mike. I am happy to leave Betsy in your hands."

"You sure you don't want to see her before you go?"

"More than anything, Mike. But it's just too dangerous. For her and for me."

"My men are good."

"I know they are. But the men we're dealing with are good, too. I don't know how they know half the things they do, and that's scary. Just keep her safe for me, that's all."

"You got it."

Teddy picked up the gear bag. "Come on, Stone. Let's get back before anyone notices we're gone."

58

Stone laid in a flight plan and took off for Teterboro.

"I hate to bail on you again," Teddy said, "but I really need more sleep."

"No problem. But you might want to put on your East Coast face."

"Aw, hell." Teddy pulled off the blond wig. "I forgot I had this on."

"There's no point trying to find this guy?"

Teddy shook his head. "We could if we wanted to take up residence, but we have other pressing matters."

"So the whole trip is a washout?"

"I wouldn't say that, Stone. We're learning more about these people. They're bicoastal, they have unlimited money, and remarkable access. They're a curious mix of Middle Eastern extremists and American thugs, and they exhibit just the type of disorganization that would result from such a mix. They're incredibly bright on the one hand, and incredibly dumb on the other.

"Take the assassination, for instance. From the surveillance tape, the assassin appears to be a Middle Eastern terrorist. Then the CIA bullet makes no sense. And if the CIA's involved, the assassination doesn't make sense. The rifle cartridge seems like an obvious plant. It's crudely done, and taken by itself it doesn't really mean anything. There's got to be more.

"Then you've got the kidnapping. The face on it is also a Middle Eastern man, the suave, clean-cut young man with the CIA credentials who lured the girl away from the dorm and got Margo Sappington to bug your phone. But the kidnapping makes little sense. Why would terrorists care if Congress passes some veterans aid bill?

"But it's all interconnected. That's why anytime we get close to making a connection, they cut and run.

"So, yes, we didn't learn anything concrete. But at least we're leaving the West Coast in disarray. Carlo Gigante will not be sending any goons to hassle Betsy again, and the connection between the extremists and the thugs has been broken."

"So what's next?" Stone said.

"Now we work from the other end. I still don't know who leaked our plans to these guys and almost got you and me killed. You and Holly both swear Ann Keaton's discreet and would not have told anyone that you had been added to the state dinner."

"That's right."

"It occurs to me there's one person she had to tell."

59

Teddy's press pass in the name of Mark Rosen got him into Congressman Carl Jenkins's office. He knew it would. A relatively unknown congressman couldn't afford to pass up an interview.

Congressman Jenkins met him at the door with a handshake and a smile. "Well now, Mr. Rosen. What can I do for you?"

Teddy's smile was apologetic. "It's about the assassination, of course. Everything's about the assassination. I understand you were personal friends with Congressman Drexel."

"We were great friends ever since we worked together on the immigration bill."

Teddy was forced to feign interest in the immigration bill, even jotted a few random notes in his notebook. "So you were seated next to him at the state dinner the night before?"

Congressman Jenkins made a face. "I was

supposed to be. At the last minute I had to give up my seat to some attorney from New York."

"You missed the state dinner?"

"More than that, I missed the last chance to see my friend."

"But you didn't know it."

"Of course."

"Did they make it up to you? Give you a rain check for another state dinner?"

"Hardly. But the White House chief of staff took me out instead."

"Isn't that Ann Keaton?"

"Yes, that's right."

"I've met her. A personable and attractive woman."

The congressman winced.

Teddy controlled his face, but a guilty reaction to Ann Keaton was exactly what he was looking for. Was it possible this harmless-looking politician was responsible for passing on the tip about Stone Barrington? He certainly had all the information. A New York lawyer rung in at the last minute at the President's request, who would be taking his place at that particular table.

Congressman Jenkins put up his hands and smiled. "Look, you're not writing this, are you?"

Teddy frowned. "What do you mean?"

"You said it was about the assassination. Because I was a friend of Congressman Drexel. Where I had dinner has nothing to do with it."

"But you missed the state dinner. As you say, your last chance to see your old friend. The fact that you didn't is poignant. Human interest."

"The fact is I missed the dinner. That may be poignant, but who I was out with is not. I'm a married man. I don't want my wife reading a story about me gallivanting around with a pretty woman instead of having dinner with my friend. That is not a fair assessment of the situation."

"I assure you, that's not what I'm writing."

Jenkins smiled. "Just between you and me, she has some boyfriend she's smitten with. She talked about him all through dinner." He put up his hand. "But don't write that, either."

"Never fear. Did he know you were out with her?"

"Yes, and he wasn't too happy about it. Not that he was jealous, don't get the wrong idea. This is all off the record, right?"

"Of course."

"Apparently she had to break a date with him to go out with me."

Teddy smiled. Congressman Jenkins had been unexpectedly helpful. He clearly wasn't the leak, but he'd given Teddy a lead.

60

If he hadn't been so cool-headed, Paul Wagner would have been worried. Margo Sappington was dead. The police were calling it a suicide, but Paul knew better. The guys he worked for had taken her out, and they'd done it because of information he'd provided. That made him at least an accessory before and after the fact. A lesser man might have been daunted.

He also might have been concerned by the fact that no one had contacted him since. It was no big deal. He hadn't called them, either. There was nothing coming out of Ann Keaton's office he couldn't read in the paper, nothing worth passing along. The assassination had thrown the President's schedule so out of whack Ann had a full-time job just juggling her appointments. Even her secretary had no time to gossip.

Teddy Fay fell into step with him as he

came out the door of the office. "Paul Wagner?"

"Yes?"

"Leonard Coleman, CIA." Teddy flashed his credentials. The ID photo matched his current appearance, which featured silver sideburns. He didn't want to be Fred Walker for this interview. "Come with me, please."

"Why?"

"Interesting reaction. That will be one of the first things we ask about. Come with me."

Teddy turned and walked away. After a moment Paul followed. Teddy never looked back. He walked down the hall with complete assurance, and opened a door to a small conference room. "In here, please."

Teddy ushered Paul in and shut the door. They sat at the table.

"You're friends with the President's chief of staff, Ann Keaton?"

"That's right."

"How did you meet?"

Paul frowned. "Hey, what is this?"

"In light of the national security threat, we're running background checks on all persons with access to the White House. Surely you understand."

"I'm not aware of any such background checks."

"Why would you be?"

"Ann would have mentioned it."

"She tells you things?"

"I'm her boyfriend."

"Yes. How'd you meet?"

"We were introduced at a party."

"Who introduced you?"

"I don't remember."

Teddy shook his head. "See, here's the problem. You're not expecting anyone to ask you that, and you should be, because you're a pro. You can't remember who introduced you because no one introduced you. You picked her up, and it was no accident. You went to the party to pick her up. You, my friend, are not who you say you are, which is a very unfortunate position to be in during a federal investigation."

Paul favored Teddy with a haughty look. Clearly this misguided agent had made a mistake.

"Who hired you?"

"No one hired me. I'm attractive to women." As if to demonstrate, he shrugged and ducked his head in the way he probably thought women found adorable. "Ann and I hit it off."

"Okay, let's take a walk."

Paul blinked. "I beg your pardon?"

"I'm going to have to take you in for

questioning. You seem like a nice guy, so I'm going to do you a favor. Walk out with me and get in the car. You don't have to sit in the back, it won't look like you're under arrest."

Teddy walked him out front where he'd left his rental car. He kept Paul distracted so he wouldn't see the diplomatic plates he'd slapped on it to keep from being towed.

Teddy pulled out and got on the highway.

"Hey," Paul said, "this isn't the way to the police station."

"Sure it is."

"No, it's not. Hey, what is this?"

Teddy took out a gun and stuck it in his ribs. "You know that car your mother always told you not to get into? This is it."

Paul's mouth fell open. "You're crazy! You're out of your mind!"

"Nonsense. Three psych evaluations cleared me to return to duty." Teddy hit the gas.

Ten miles out of town Teddy spotted an abandoned service station. He turned in, drove around to the back, and put the car in park. "Get out."

Paul hesitated. Teddy prodded him with the gun. Paul got out. Teddy kept the gun trained on him, and made sure they couldn't be seen from the road.

"All right," Teddy said. "Let's start again. You don't want to tell me so I'll tell you. You were hired to romance Ann Keaton and learn anything you could. Ann broke a date with you to take care of a congressman who got bumped from the state dinner to make room for Stone Barrington. You didn't think it was particularly important, but you passed the information along. It turned out it actually was. Gunmen tried to take out Stone Barrington, but missed. Not your fault, but you got bad points on your side of the ledger. You're associated with a failure. But you don't know that, so you're not worried about it.

"You also told them that Holly Barker had been talking to Margo Sappington."

Paul's eyes flicked.

"Yes, I thought so. And that bothers you, because she wound up dead."

"She committed suicide."

"Cut the crap. You're not that naïve. You're not just playing secret agent anymore, you're involved in a murder. Lucky for you, there's an easy way out. All you have to do is cooperate."

Teddy stuck his gun back in his pocket and turned to the car.

Paul lunged.

To his surprise, the older, less athletic-looking man lowered his shoulder and spun to the right, trapping Paul's wrist with one hand while grabbing his elbow with the other. Teddy twisted hard in a bone-snapping move.

With a yowl of pain, Paul swung sideways and leaped, not at Teddy as he had intended, but toward the service station wall. He crashed headfirst into the bricks and fell to the dirt in a misshapen heap.

Paul's head was twisted at an impossible angle. Teddy didn't even have to feel his pulse to know he was dead.

Teddy shook his head and sighed.

All right, how did he deal with this?

61

"Did you kill Ann Keaton's boyfriend?" Stone Barrington asked accusingly.

Teddy paused. "Ann's boyfriend had an accident," he said eventually. "His car went off a bridge. These things happen. How did you know about that anyway?"

"Ann called me last night, hysterical, because her boyfriend was killed in an accident. Only it wasn't an accident, was it? These things don't just happen. You *make* them happen."

"It really was an accident. Maybe not a car wreck, but close enough."

"Teddy."

"Ann's boyfriend was a mercenary, hired to pump her for information."

"I can't believe that."

"He's the answer to the million-dollar question of how those guys got on to you so fast. The President tells Ann to get Stone Barrington. Ann breaks a date with lover

boy to set it up and babysit the congressman whose seat you took. That's how they
knew."

"He told you that?"

"He wouldn't tell me anything. He was
one of those handsome, dumb, arrogant
types who think they can walk on water. If
he hadn't tried to kill me, he'd still be alive."

"If you wanted him to be, he'd still be
alive. Wasn't he worth keeping around just
to pump for information?"

"He didn't have any. He was a low-level
functionary who didn't even know who
hired him. He wasn't going to give us
anything. On the other hand, he could blow
our whole covert operation just by telling
the wrong people what we're asking."

"So you set him up."

Teddy shrugged. "Maybe a little."

Stone sighed and shook his head. "Take it
easy, will you? You're leaving a trail of bodies
in your wake."

"That's the nature of the beast."

"Even so. Sooner or later someone's going
to notice."

62

Mike Freeman pulled to a stop behind the row of police cars lining the top of the bluff. He spotted his friend on the force and wandered over.

"Where is he?"

"Down there."

Down there was the base of the cliff where the body had been discovered floating in the bay. No one much wanted to climb down, and the cops were all standing around waiting for the gurney to be hoisted up by the crane on the wrecker ordered by the emergency rescue team. Not that there was any rescuing to be done. The man was way past help. The body was merely being retrieved for the cops.

Mike walked up to the edge of the cliff, looked over, and saw the gurney bumping up the side of the canyon wall far below. He felt slightly queasy, and backed away from the edge.

The cop grinned at him. "Join the club. No one wants to supervise the hoist. We all decided we could damn well wait."

The gurney cleared the edge of the cliff. The crane swung it over and set it down.

Homicide detectives were waiting to pounce. They were beaten out by the doctor, who somehow managed to insert himself next to the gurney and look just as if he'd ridden up with it. Mike figured that was probably for the benefit of the TV cameras.

Mike squeezed in as close as he could. He wanted to see for himself if it was really Carlo Gigante. It certainly figured to be. His goons had been found dead next to his car in the Palm Palace parking lot. They were unlikely to have been killed for their own sake. Their boss's corpse could not be far behind.

"That looks like him from his picture," Mike said. "Is it him?"

The cop looked. "Yeah, that's him."

"Thanks."

Mike whipped out his cell phone and called Stone Barrington.

Teddy relayed the information to Holly Barker.

"He took out Carlo Gigante?" Holly said.

"Yes."

"Why?"

"Either he thought Carlo could lead us to him, or he's just plain mean."

"Do you think Gigante knew his address?"

"No."

"So the odds favor just plain mean."

"That's the interesting thing about the West Coast connection. He, of all people, is the most likely card-carrying terrorist."

"Why do you say that?" Holly said.

"He has links to extremists. When they needed a hit man on short notice, he had no problem coming up with an ISIS recruit, the student from UCLA."

"He also hired Gigante."

"He's open-minded. He doesn't discriminate. The point is he has the connections. Our East Coast kidnapper only seems to hire American thugs."

"Except for the shooter."

"He's the exception that proves the rule. But he kind of has to be. If you want an assassin, you need to train your own sniper."

"Unless he's an embittered Iraq War vet with post-traumatic stress disorder."

Teddy shrugged. "That would fit in with the veterans aid bill. But we've pretty well established that the shooter is the man in the surveillance footage."

Holly exhaled. "We keep going around in circles."

"Yes, but we're picking up stuff on every turn. And we're throwing monkey wrenches into their machinery. We may be frustrated by our progress, but I doubt if these guys are very happy with how things are going either."

63

Abdul-Hakim bit the bullet and made the call. "I heard from our contact on the West Coast. There was a leak. It's been plugged."

Calvin Hancock's voice was cold. "That is not what I want to hear."

"No, it's good news. That idiot Gigante cracked and gave up my contact. Before it could come back to bite us, my contact stepped in and shut him up."

"Gigante?"

"Yes."

"We lost our source on the coast?"

"We have several. We lost one. It shouldn't matter at this point."

"We also lost our source in the White House."

"He was no use to us. We'd already pulled the plug."

"That's not the point. The point is we're being outplayed. As long as that's the case, we're not in charge. I like to be in charge."

"I know."

"What was that?" Calvin said sharply.

"I agree. It's bad. What do you want to do?"

"The Speaker hasn't budged since you hung up on him. He hasn't been back to the White House. He hasn't been on TV."

"Do you want me to nudge him again?"

"It will do no good. Someone sold him on demanding proof of life. We can't get into a game of calling each other's bluff. I need the Speaker in my pocket. People are going to start pushing him, hard. I need him standing firm, or this whole thing collapses."

"I understand," Abdul-Hakim said. "What do you want me to do?"

64

Abdul-Hakim pulled up in front of the cabin. He took the copy of the *Washington Post* off the passenger seat, got out, and went up the step. The front door was unlocked. He pushed it open, stepped inside.

The big man was sitting on the couch playing solitaire. He seemed to be lost in concentration. He glanced up at Abdul-Hakim and went back to his game.

"Where is she?"

He waved his hand without even looking up. "Back there."

"Are you sure?"

"She's hurt, she's weak, there's nowhere to go. She's tied up, too."

"With rope?"

"Yeah."

Abdul-Hakim walked across the room and parted the curtain that served as a door, and looked in the back room.

Karen lay on the mattress on the floor.

She was not in good shape. Her finger had become infected, and she was running a fever. She was curled up in a fetal position and her eyes were closed, as if trying to will the world away.

Abdul-Hakim stepped back into the front room. "Get her up."

The big man looked at him. "Huh?"

"Get her up and bring her out."

"You don't want to just do her in there?"

Abdul-Hakim took a breath. "I'm not shooting her. Just get her up."

The big man grunted and heaved a sigh. He set the deck of cards on the table and clambered to his feet from the low couch. He pushed his way through the curtain and into the back room.

He had a paranoid flash that the girl was gone, that it was like the old joke where the customer tells the waiter to try the soup and there's no spoon. But, no, there she was, just like he had left her.

He bent down and rolled her over. "Get up."

She rolled back and curled up, facing away.

The big man wasn't putting up with that nonsense. He hefted her up, slung her over his shoulder, and carried her out.

"I said get her up, not lift her up," Abdul-

Hakim said. "I need her awake. Untie her."

The big man flopped her on the couch and took the ropes off.

"Stand her up."

He wrestled her to her feet, but she didn't stand, just hung like deadweight.

There was a pitcher of water next to the washbasin. Abdul-Hakim picked it up, tossed it in Karen's face.

"Hey. That's my water."

"You'll get more tomorrow."

Karen blew water out of her mouth, blinked her eyes, glared up at the two men.

"Good, you're awake," Abdul-Hakim said.

Karen sagged in the big man's arms.

"Can you stand? You're not going to like it if you can't. Stand her up."

The big man pulled her up straight.

"Let go of her."

He did.

Karen fell to the floor.

"Stand her up again."

He dragged her to her feet.

"You like falling on the floor? We're going to keep standing you up until you don't. It's not that I think you're faking. I think you're not trying. Let her go."

Karen swayed, but stayed on her feet.

"Good."

Abdul-Hakim took the copy of the *Wash-*

ington Post, thrust it into her hands. "Hold it up. Next to your face. Not in front of your face, next to it. Straighten it out so the date shows."

Karen held the paper.

Abdul-Hakim whipped out his cell phone, snapped the picture. He checked the phone to make sure it would do. He nodded. "Put her back."

The big man scooped her up, carried her into the back room.

Abdul Hakim punched the number into the phone and forwarded the photo to Congressman Blaine.

65

Kevin Cushman, aka Warplord924, burst into Holly's office. "We got it!"

Holly looked up in surprise. So did the director of Homeland Security, with whom she was meeting.

"Sorry, ma'am," Kevin said. "I didn't realize someone was here. I fixed that computer virus I couldn't isolate, but I won't bother you with that now."

Kevin ducked back into the computer room, closing the door behind him.

Holly barely listened while the director of Homeland Security droned on. The issue was access to the President, which he wasn't getting. Holly wished he wasn't getting access to her.

Finally she managed to ease him out the door. She hurried to see what was up with Kevin.

"All right, what's so damn important?" she demanded.

Kevin pointed at the computer screen. On it was an enlargement of the cell phone photo Abdul-Hakim had taken of Karen Blaine. The resolution was high, the date on the paper was clear.

"This photo was just forwarded to Speaker Blaine. Along with the text message **Pass the bill**. The picture was sent from an unlisted cell phone approximately seventy-five miles northwest of here. It was clearly taken in a cabin of some sort. There are woodlands in that area where a cabin might be."

"Can you pin it down?"

"Not with any accuracy. You're talking about a ten-mile radius, if you're lucky. It could be more. And there's no guarantee the photo was sent from where it was taken."

"Is there anything helpful in the photo itself?"

"Not that I can tell. The cabin's pretty bare. You can only tell it's a cabin because the walls are unfinished. It's not insulated, which means it's not heated at all, unless there's a wood-burning fireplace. So there's probably no running water. If there is, it's shut off in the winter. Of course, the whole cabin would be shut down in the winter."

"Does any of that help pinpoint the location?"

"No."

Teddy came in and Kevin went through the whole spiel again.

"All right," Teddy said. "We still can't find her, but at least we know she's alive."

"It's a twenty-mile area," Holly said. "We could flood it with agents."

"The girl would be dead before they were even briefed. There's no such thing as a clandestine operation. If we move against these people, they'll know it."

"We can't do nothing."

"We're not. We're playing their game. And they blinked. They want this to happen. Why, we don't know, but they want it enough to keep the girl alive. If we keep pressing them for proof, we can keep them on the defensive, and help pin the location down."

"Yeah, but how can we do that?" Holly said. "The Speaker doesn't contact them, they contact him."

"Right. We'd have to make them want something."

"What could they possibly want?"

"An explanation," Teddy said. "We'd have to get the Speaker to do something they didn't ask him to do."

"Like what?"

"I don't know. The guy's a basket case. I

don't know how he's holding it together."

The phone rang. They looked around, but it was on the computer. A call to Speaker Blaine's phone.

"Oh, my God," Holly said. "Do you suppose we just got lucky?"

The Speaker answered on the second ring. "Hello?"

It wasn't the kidnappers. That was clear from the opening line.

"What the hell do you think you're doing?"

"Who is this?"

"Who is this? You don't recognize my voice?"

"Herman?"

"Who else would it be?" Herman Foster said. "And do you know what I'm doing? I'm making one of those calls we always make when there's about to be a crucial vote. I just never expected to be making one to you."

"Herman —"

"Guess who I just got a call from? Calvin Hancock. He read me the riot act, told me to get you in line. That's a good one, isn't it? When *I* have to tell *you*."

"You don't understand."

"I understand perfectly well. You want a bipartisan vote. I couldn't believe the words

286

were coming out of your mouth. Well, it's not too late to fix it. All you have to do is go on TV, explain your previous statement, and urge us to kill the bill. Just like that, you'll be back in charge."

"It's not that easy."

"Oh, is that right? Well, you better make it that easy. If this bill passes, everyone will be blaming you."

Herman Foster hung up the phone, looked at the man sitting across from him. "How was that?"

Calvin Hancock leaned back in his desk chair. "That's perfect, Herman," Calvin said. "The Speaker's getting too big for his britches, putting his interests above the party. No one is above the party. Are you ready to come down on him again if I give the call?"

"Of course."

"I hope it doesn't come to that."

"I hope so, too. But if it does, I'm ready."

Calvin got to his feet, extended his hand. "Good man."

Herman Foster accepted his dismissal with good grace. One always did with Calvin Hancock. The best strategy was to figure out what the man wanted, and get there first. Herman had done it well enough to have been bankrolled in the last two elections. He exited the room, closing the heavy wood door behind him.

As soon as he was gone, Calvin Hancock snatched up the phone, punched in a number.

The call was answered on the first ring.

"Yes?" Abdul-Hakim said.

"Start Phase Two."

66

Abdul-Hakim drove the gray van up to the garage. He got out, unlocked the padlock, raised the door. He drove the van in, hopped out, switched on the lights, and pulled the door down behind him.

He had a moment of panic when he heard nothing in the empty garage. Then the hum of the freezer reassured him. He walked over to it, raised the lid.

The body of the dead sniper lay crumpled up inside. A thin layer of frost gave him a surreal look.

Abdul-Hakim nodded in satisfaction. He opened the back of the van and rolled out a gurney. He released the lever, pulled it up to full height, and rolled it over to the freezer. He took the body out and laid it on top of the gurney. The corpse was stiff and bent at the waist and wouldn't lie flat. When he pushed the legs down, it actually sat up.

Abdul-Hakim exhaled noisily. This wasn't

going to work. He pushed the body back down, which flipped its legs up again. He ignored them and secured the torso to the gurney with straps. He rolled it into the shadows at the back wall and left it there, with the legs still sticking straight up.

He drove the van out of the garage, switched off the lights, and locked the door. He drove around, parked the van on the street, went into a diner and had lunch. He picked his way through a club sandwich, topped it off with a piece of blueberry pie. He lingered over coffee, checked his watch. It had probably been long enough.

Abdul-Hakim paid his check, and drove the van back to the garage.

Abdul-Hakim rolled the gurney out from the wall and positioned it under the overhead light. While not entirely thawed, the corpse was at least pliable. He was able to pull the legs flat on the gurney, which was a vast improvement. He rolled the body over and laid it on its stomach.

He got the medical bag from the van and went to work. With scalpel, clamps, and forceps he began digging for the bullet.

It wasn't easy. The shot had gone through the back of the skull, and the bone was hard. He should have brought a hammer. He wondered if there was anything similar in the doctor's bag. There was. A wooden mallet, not as heavy as he would have liked, but better than nothing. He banged on the scalpel, wiggled it around, enlarged the hole. Finally there came the satisfying rasp of metal on metal. He'd found it. Now to get it out.

He butchered the job removing the bullet. He'd been told it didn't matter, still he hated to do such poor work. It just went against the grain. But he had neither the equipment nor the expertise to do better. He dug it out, popped it into a plastic Ziploc bag. Later he'd make sure to throw it away.

Now the hand.

Abdul-Hakim positioned the body on the gurney so the left arm lay flat from elbow to fingertips, palm down. He took a surgical saw from the doctor's bag and cut the hand off at the wrist. It was amazingly easy. The fact that the body was still somewhat frozen actually helped. He put the severed hand in another Ziploc bag.

When he was done he rolled the gurney back to the van and loaded the body in. He closed up the van, locked the garage, and left.

He was back at one in the morning. He picked up the van and drove to a bar in the suburbs. As the van pulled up, three men dressed in black came out of the bar and climbed into the back. Once they were aboard, the van took off for Falls Church, Virginia.

There was no traffic at that time of night, and he arrived at his destination in thirty minutes. He drove by the house, double-checked the address, circled the block and came up on the house again. Before he reached it he pulled off into the shadows and cut the engine.

In the back of the van the three men in black propped up the dead sniper and strapped him into a suicide bomber's vest. It wasn't armed, still they handled it gingerly. When they were done, they laid him down on the floor of the van.

Abdul-Hakim got out of the cab, came back to inspect their work. It met with his approval. He nodded to the man designated for the next task.

The man slipped out of the van, crept through the shadows to a private home down the street. There was a car parked in the driveway. The man stole up to the car, slipped a Slim Jim into the driver's side window. Moments later the door lock clicked.

The man in black eased the door open,

reached onto the floor for the release, and popped the trunk.

The van pulled up alongside. Two men in black got out, unloaded the dead sniper, and lifted him into the trunk.

Abdul-Hakim hopped out of the van, armed the suicide bomber's vest, and closed the trunk.

He took the severed hand out of the Ziploc bag and wedged it under the driver's seat. After the explosion, he wanted this small piece of Salih's anatomy intact.

He locked the car, got back in the van, and circled the block. He parked in the same spot in the shadows where he'd been before, and settled down to wait.

67

Herman Foster checked his voice mail. He had thirteen new messages, something to be expected after having sounded the clarion call. He skimmed them to see if any were important.

They weren't. Some he deleted as soon as he recognized the voice. Some he saved without listening to them. During a lull, he might play them later.

Only one actually made the cut. Ironically, it was one he would have deleted if his hands hadn't been occupied cutting his pancakes. That was from Congressman Greely, a stodgy old bore who merited no consideration whatsoever because he never had the gumption to do anything except vote the straight party line. Herman Foster was just reaching for the delete button when he heard him say, ". . . I wondered if there was something wrong with the Speaker. He's never canceled a dinner before, and I wondered if you'd heard anything."

Herman Foster could think of any number of reasons to cancel a dinner with Congressman Greely, though it was unlike Congressman Blaine to miss a commitment. The Speaker was always the flesh-pressing type of politician, shaking hands and kissing babies.

Foster called Greely back. That was probably a first for him, calling the congressman. But if Speaker Blaine was canceling dinner appointments, that was something Calvin Hancock would want to know.

"Marty, it's Herman. Got your message."

"Yes, yes. Speaker Blaine was coming to dinner last night and he canceled, and I'm concerned because it's not like him. And there's been all this talk about the veterans aid bill and bipartisanship and you can't turn on the TV without hearing —"

"Marty. What did he say?"

"He said he didn't feel well. And this is a man who showed up to vote with viral pneumonia."

"When did he cancel?"

"Last night. At the last minute. Alice was already cooking. It was like he'd forgotten all about it, made other plans, then realized he was coming to dinner. I'm worried about him. If he's getting forgetful, it's something the party will have to deal with."

"Okay, thanks for calling."

Herman Foster hung up the phone. This was not good. He'd have to call Calvin Hancock. Not now, it was too early, but soon. This was the type of situation that would get worse the longer he sat on it.

Foster's pancakes had gotten cold. He pushed the plate back, grabbed his briefcase, and went out the door.

He was halfway to his car before he realized he hadn't said goodbye to his wife. She, as was her custom, had made him breakfast and gone back to bed. He wasn't about to turn around now. He'd apologize this evening.

Foster unlocked the car, tossed his briefcase on the passenger seat, climbed in, and started the engine.

In the gray van down the street, Abdul-Hakim pressed the button on the remote control detonator.

Foster heard a faint beeping noise. He wondered what it was.

The car exploded.

68

The President's national security briefing had virtually the same cast as it had for the assassination of Congressman Drexel. The new addition was the demolitions expert from the bomb squad, though it would be a while before he got a chance to talk. Clyde Benedict, the director of Homeland Security, was holding forth.

"Madam President, this is no longer an isolated incident. We are now talking about a coordinated terrorist attack against members of the United States Congress."

"Despite the fact we have one sniper and one suicide bomber?" Kate said.

"Despite that. I think the situation is clear."

"The situation is anything but clear," Lance Cabot said. "Sorry to interrupt, Madam President, but there are only what can be described as special circumstances."

"What special circumstances?"

"This is demolitions expert Roger Mc-Clarey. He's done an analysis of what remains of the device, and his findings are interesting. Mr. McClarey?"

Roger McClarey cleared his throat. "The device used was your typical suicide vest, several separate charges designed to go off simultaneously, any one blast triggering the others. It is not a particularly sophisticated device, which is why it is popular. It could be detonated by a button wired to a single chamber."

"That was done in this case?" Kate said.

"Apparently."

"Then what's the problem?" Clyde Benedict chimed in.

"Most suicide bombings fit a pattern. The bomber walks into a crowd where the bomb would do the most damage, and detonates."

"In this case he was targeting a particular person."

"Even so. He would walk up to him and detonate. He wouldn't care where that was. He would pick the easiest access with the most possibility of success. He wouldn't worry about collateral damage. In most instances, it would be the icing on the cake."

The director scoffed at the logic. "So he blew him up at home. That's where he knew he'd be."

Roger shook his head. "That doesn't make it easier, it makes it harder. You go to his office building, wait for him to arrive. When he walks into the lobby, you blow him up. Simple.

"Your way, the congressman comes out his front door. A lone man approaches him. Someone he doesn't know. A congressman's already been killed, which puts him on his guard. Is he going to stand there and let an unknown man walk up to him?"

"That's not what happened here."

"No, it isn't. The bomber waited in his car. All night, most likely, since after daybreak he would have been seen. To the best we can determine, which is hard since the whole car was blown apart, he curled up and hid in the trunk. He waited there all night for the congressman to wake up and start his car. When the car started, he detonated his bomb.

"The trunk is the worst possible place to put the bomb. You know you blow yourself up, but you can't be sure of your target, though in this case enough explosive was used for any reasonable certainty. Still, it makes no sense. If you want to blow someone up when they start the car, you wire the ignition. This is not rocket science. Two-bit gangsters have been doing it since Prohibition."

"You find that convincing?" the director said. "Car bombs can fail. When they do, you can't do anything about it. If a suicide vest fails, a bomber on the spot can deal with it and find another way to detonate."

"Do we know who this bomber is?" Holly Barker asked, trying to cut short the argument.

"We do not. We managed to save a fragment of a fingerprint and get a sufficient DNA sample to determine his probable ethnic origin."

"Can you do that?"

"It's not an exact science, but there are a few markers we can use as indicators," Lance said. "The body was obliterated, but we were lucky enough to recover almost an entire hand. Tests are still being run, but preliminary results indicate the bomber to be of Middle Eastern ancestry."

"So the sniper and the bomber are both Middle Eastern," the director of Homeland Security said.

"That goes no further than this room," Kate Lee said. "We will be releasing a statement, of course, but a preliminary finding of that sort would be highly inflammatory, resulting in widespread speculation and panic. We have yet to confirm the identity of the shooter, and our investigation into the bombing has barely begun."

"I want all the details of the investigation, evidence, and up-to-the-minute findings forwarded to me at my office," Holly said.

Lance gave her a look. "May I remind you you're not running the CIA."

"I'm briefing the President. If we have to convene a meeting like this every time there's a new development, the government will shut down."

"Well done," Kate Lee said as Holly walked her back to the Oval Office. "Any meetings of this type that you can keep me out of I will greatly appreciate."

"I understand. What do you think of the theory about the bomber?"

"It makes sense. It's not helpful, but it makes sense."

"It is a strange method for a suicide bomber." Holly took a breath. "Madam President, I know you don't like to play the mommy card, but if you'd like to grab some time with your son, why don't you let me run interference and you take some now before things get crazy?"

Kate smiled. "I wish I could."

"Why can't you?"

"I have to reassure the American public."

69

Teddy Fay, Holly Barker, and Millie Martindale watched Kate's speech in Holly's office. Kevin left the connecting door open and watched it, too. Not that he couldn't have streamed it on his computer, but he liked being part of the group.

Kate didn't dwell on any of the inconsistencies of the bombing. She just presented a simple, direct picture. The United States had been the victim of a terrorist attack. The President had declared a state of emergency. All agencies were on high alert. These were the normal, sensible precautions taken at such times to protect the American people.

At the end of the President's speech all the reporters began shouting at once, even though the President was not taking questions. As she turned to walk away, one voice could be heard above the rest. "Does this mean you're shutting down Congress?"

"That's the question, isn't it?" Millie said. "If the vote never comes to the floor, what happens to the Speaker's daughter?"

"Does the President know about her?" Kevin blurted.

They all looked at him.

"See, this is what is meant by a need-to-know basis," Teddy said.

Kevin put up his hands. "Oh, no, no, no. I didn't ask a thing. I was just wondering aloud. I'll stop wondering."

"Can you hear the phone from in here?" Holly said.

"Yes, I can. And even if I couldn't, it's being recorded."

"But you wouldn't know it had been."

"Are you kidding me? When a call comes in, a giant picture of Alexander Graham Bell's phone fills the screen. It stays there until I click it away. Trust me, I'm not missing any calls."

The phone rang.

Kevin sprinted for the computer. The others followed him in.

Alexander Graham Bell's phone was indeed displayed on the screen. Kevin clicked it away, revealing the decibel bars of the sound program.

The Speaker's voice came over the phone. It quavered, as if he'd gotten up off his deathbed to answer. "Hello?"

Abdul-Hakim's voice was ominous. "Don't let them postpone the vote."

There was a moment's shocked silence while the words sunk in. "How can I do that?" Blaine wailed. "I have no control over that. I can make sure the bill passes when the vote is taken. I have the votes. You have nothing to fear.

"But when it's voted on? How can I control that? They could postpone the vote, or decide to recess. The President could suspend Congress. It was hard before. Now another congressman has been killed. What do you expect to happen? I can control my party, but I can't control what Congress does in the midst of a national emergency."

"I don't think you understand," Abdul-Hakim said evenly. There was a pause before he spoke again, and when he did it was not into the phone. "Say hello."

The tentative, fearful, hoarse voice of Karen Blaine came over the wire. "Daddy?"

"Karen! Karen!"

Karen suddenly screamed and dropped the phone. She could be heard sobbing in the background as it was picked up from the cabin floor.

"If the vote is postponed, she dies," Abdul-Hakim said, and hung up.

304

70

Teddy, Holly, and Millie conferred in Holly's office while Kevin traced the call.

"Okay," Teddy said. "The vote's scheduled for tomorrow afternoon. We've got to make sure it happens, and we've got to find Karen Blaine by then. Once the vote is over, they have no reason to keep her alive any longer no matter what the result."

"Then we have to tell the CIA," Holly said.

"That's the other way we get her killed. Then they won't wait till tomorrow afternoon. If it were as easy as telling the CIA, I wouldn't be here and the President would have done so at the start."

"Well, we can't just wait around for them to kill her."

"Got it!" Kevin called.

They trooped into the other room.

"Well?" Teddy demanded.

"Much better," Kevin said. "The Speaker

kept him on the phone. I was able to narrow the search, particularly as it's the same area as before." He clicked the mouse, brought up the map with a ten-mile radius circle. "We were able to narrow the area down from this . . . to this." He clicked the mouse, and a smaller circle appeared. The center was somewhat west of the center of the larger circle.

"It moved," Holly said.

"It didn't move. It's just more accurate. We had a ten-mile radius. Now we have a radius of three-point-five being generated from a nucleus four-tenths of a mile west and two-tenths of a mile south of what we originally predicted."

"And this one is accurate and the other one isn't?"

"They're both accurate. This is *more* accurate."

"So we're talking about an area seven miles wide."

"That's right."

"You have a map of it?"

"Partial."

"What do you mean 'partial'?"

"Not all roads are named or mapped. There are three or four hundred homes listed, and there will be more cabins that aren't."

"Okay," Teddy said. "That's doable. I can eliminate most of these houses on sight. We're talking a primitive cabin here. I'll drive around and check them out."

"All night?" Holly said.

"No. You can't disguise your headlights on a dead-end dirt road. I can eliminate the houses on the main drag, but what we're looking for will take daylight."

"You'll never do it in time," Holly said. "Not unless you luck onto the kidnappers first thing. By the time you get up there you'll only have a couple of hours of daylight left. You're better off driving up before dawn. If the vote's tomorrow afternoon, you're really racing the clock. If the vote's not tomorrow afternoon . . ."

"That's up to you. Get the President not to suspend Congress and not to postpone the vote."

"How do I do that?"

"Any way you can. You're the national security advisor. Tell her it's in the interests of national security."

"That's a tough sell."

"Get Stone Barrington to help you. He has the ear of the President, and I imagine Speaker Blaine will be making a pitch of his own."

"Let them handle the President, then,"

Holly said. "I'll go with you."

"You can't."

"You need help."

"I'll go," Millie Martindale said.

"You can't go," Holly said.

"Why not?"

"These guys play rough."

Millie stuck out her chin. "So do I."

"Do you have a gun?" Teddy said.

"Not on me."

"That's not a problem," Teddy said. "What about a permit?"

"I have one at home. I can get it."

"No need. If I could borrow Holly's computer."

"Could we try to limit the number of felonies perpetrated on national security equipment?" Holly said.

Teddy reached into his jacket and took out one of the guns he'd requisitioned from the CIA. He turned it around, offered the butt to Millie. "Can you use this?"

Millie took the gun, popped the safety on and off, slid out the magazine, made sure it was loaded. She chambered a round, looked at it critically. "It'll do."

"Okay," Teddy said. "We'll start at four in the morning, separate cars, burner phones. You take the east, I'll take the west. We'll move in from the south, and check out every cabin it could possibly be."

"Check out how?"

"Knock on the door and go in."

"If they refuse?"

"Don't take no for an answer. Flash your ID. You're CIA, aren't you?"

"I thought we weren't involving the CIA."

"Not officially. I'm talking about us. If it's pay dirt it won't matter. If it's not, you'll have moved on before the word gets around."

"What if no one's home?"

"Break a window and go in."

"I don't like it," Holly said.

"I hate it like hell, but there we are," Teddy said.

"No, I don't like her going alone."

"I'll go," Kevin said. He looked scared out of his mind, had obviously made the offer because it seemed the gentlemanly thing to do.

"We need you here in case there's another call. To narrow the search." Teddy thought a moment, looked at Millie. "Your FBI boyfriend."

"Quentin?"

"You trust him?"

"Yes, I trust him. You should use him."

"If we do, it will be on a very limited basis. He'll be brought in for one specific assignment. And I won't brief him. He won't meet me at all."

"So, when you say trust . . ." Millie said ironically.

"Don't get snippy. Your feelings aren't the issue here." Teddy clapped his hands together. "Okay, we've all got our marching orders. Holly, line up Stone Barrington. Millie, line up your young man, but not here. Keep him away from this office."

"I'll see him in my apartment. He'll be more pliable."

"Excellent."

"What are you going to do?"

"Instruct Kevin on the maps we need and make plans."

Teddy said it with complete assurance.

He wished it were so simple.

"Stone, it's Holly Barker."

"Holly. How are you?"

"I've had two congressmen killed on my watch, how do you think?"

"It's not your job to stop assassinations."

"No, it's my job to advise the President. She just declared a national emergency, and that doesn't make my advice look very good."

"Do I really need to point out the flaws in that logic?"

"No, but I need your help."

"Name it."

"I'm afraid the President's going to shut down Congress, in spite of the fact the kidnappers threatened to kill the girl. I need you to talk her out of it."

"She won't listen to you?"

"I'm dealing with her at arm's length. I think you know why. You, on the other hand, can broach certain subjects."

Stone's phone beeped. "Hang on. I got another call." He put Holly on hold, pressed the button to answer.

"Stone. It's Ann Keaton, calling for the President."

"Ann. I thought you'd be taking time off."

"It's a national emergency, I'm on the job. Can you come?"

"When?"

"Now. Come right over."

"Be right there." Stone switched back to Holly Barker. "We're in luck. The President wants to see me."

"That isn't just luck, is it?"

"No."

Stone hung up on Holly and called his hotel's front desk. "It's Stone Barrington. I need a limo to the White House."

"Yes, sir. When do you need it?"

"Five minutes."

The limo was waiting when Stone came out the door. It whisked him to the White House. His name had not only been left at security, but a Secret Service agent was waiting to escort him to the Oval Office.

Speaker Blaine was already there. His struggled to his feet, clung to Stone as if to a lifeline.

Kate made a helpless gesture behind Blaine's back.

"Stone, thank goodness you're here," Blaine said. "We need your help. I've heard from the kidnappers."

"What do they say?"

"They say if we postpone the vote, they'll kill my daughter."

"That's out of your control."

"I tried to tell them that, but they don't care. They put Karen on the phone. She screamed." The Speaker dissolved into tears and sank down on the couch.

"I've already addressed the American people," Kate said. "Congress has recessed for the day. Everyone expects it to be suspended tomorrow. I'd have to go on TV and make a case why it shouldn't be."

"Do it! Do it!" the Speaker cried in anguish.

"What's your opinion at this point? Are they bluffing or would they really kill her?" Kate said.

"The only way to find out is a curt refusal."

"No!" Blaine wailed.

"Personally, I don't think they will," Stone said. "They've got too much invested."

"You think I should postpone?"

"No, I don't. These people are unpredictable and may decide keeping a hostage isn't worth it if the vote doesn't move forward

313

on schedule."

The Speaker looked up at Stone with watery eyes. "Thank you."

"Go home. Wait for another call."

"What if I get one?"

"Let us know."

"No, what do I tell them?"

"Tell them it's all right, you've talked to the President."

"It's all right?"

"However you want to phrase it. You've talked to the President, it's taken care of. Sit tight and wait for the vote. Go on, now. Get back home."

The Speaker went out.

As soon as he was gone, Kate said, "Is that really your opinion?"

"It is. Not that I trust it. There's been something wrong with this thing from the word go. It's a kidnapping *and* a terrorist attack. Now you have three separate things. A kidnapping and a shooting and a bomb-ing."

"But you think I should urge Congress to vote?"

"Don't go by just me," Stone said. "You should get as many opinions as possible."

"I know. There aren't that many people I can ask."

"I know."

"I'd like to talk to Holly," Kate said. Her eyes sought his. "I wish it were possible."

Stone betrayed nothing. "It must be very frustrating."

"You have no idea."

"You still haven't told Will?"

Kate made a face. "You know I can't. For Karen Blaine's safety I've had to keep this close to the chest."

Stone took a breath. "Madam President, you're doing the right thing. What's important at this point is to give the Speaker's daughter as much time as we can, and let the kidnappers know it. If you're not going to suspend Congress, go on TV and say so."

"What do I do then?"

"Trust that other people have your back."

72

"My fellow Americans. I know it seems like I just addressed you, but I have an important update, and I want you to hear it now.

"We have never bowed to terrorism. We do not negotiate with terrorists. We do not allow terrorists to dictate what we can and cannot do.

"Many believe Congress will be suspended tomorrow. I have considered the idea of shutting it down out of respect for the congressmen who have died. But if we do that, the terrorists win. They will have taken control of our government. They will be dictating what our Congress may or may not do.

"Congress will be in session tomorrow, proudly defiant in the face of adversity, a glowing beacon of democracy. I am certain in my heart that is what Congressman Drexel and Congressman Foster would have wanted, instead of the hollow gesture of shutting down the very institution they so dearly loved.

"I am therefore directing Congress to resume session tomorrow and proceed with all usual business."

73

Quentin Phillips smiled and kissed Millie Martindale when she let him into her apartment. Millie had invited him to dinner, and he was looking forward to food, sex, and a chance to pump her for information.

He looked around and frowned quizzically. "You're not cooking?"

"No, I thought we'd order something."

Quentin put his arms around her waist, pulled her to him.

There was a knock on the door.

"Damn," Quentin said. "Whoever that is, get rid of them. Unless it's the food."

"I haven't ordered yet."

Millie went to the door.

Holly Barker came in.

Quentin's expression was priceless. Holly was the last person he expected to see, and someone he couldn't throw out. He had worked with Holly before, and been instrumental in aiding in the capture of the sultan's twin sons.

"Ah, good, you're already here," Holly said. "Has Millie told you anything?"

"No. Why?"

"Quentin, I need you for a special assignment."

"I'm not CIA."

"It's not a CIA operation. It's classified, and you can't tell anyone about it, including the FBI."

"I'd have to get clearance from my immediate superior."

"Then you're out," Holly said. She turned to go.

"Don't be obtuse," Millie said. "This is probably the most important assignment you've ever been offered. You're going to turn it down?"

"What is it?"

"I can't tell you unless you're in," Holly said. "Which is why you're out. I need you to commit to it sight unseen."

"He's your man," Millie said. "Let me work on him."

"We don't have that kind of time. Quentin, the only reason I'm not out that door is there isn't time to dig up someone else. You worked with me on the sleeper cells. Do you think I'd steer you wrong?"

"All right, I'm in. What have we got?"

"A girl's been kidnapped. We've pinned down the location where she's being held to this area."

Holly unfolded a map and slapped it down on the kitchen table. Kevin had mocked it up just for Quentin. A black line divided the search area into what appeared to be two equal halves but was actually two of three thirds. The western third, which was Teddy's search area, didn't appear on this map.

"Wait a minute," Quentin said. "This isn't about the terrorist attack?"

"No."

"Is that why you wanted me to agree to it first? Because you thought I'd turn it down?"

"Let her tell you what it is," Millie said impatiently.

Holly pointed to the map. "The cabin where she's being held is in this area. We need to find her, and fast. By tomorrow she will probably be dead."

"Why?"

"They'll kill her," Millie said. "That's why I need help. I can't cover the whole area myself. If you help me, we cut the time in half."

"If time's so urgent, why just the two of us?"

Millie started to flare up again, but Holly said, "That's a legitimate question. The kidnappers will kill the girl if there's any official involvement. That's why I can't use the CIA."

"You don't think the CIA can be discreet?"

"The kidnappers would know. I don't know how they'd know, but they'd know. I've been told not to take a chance."

"By the President?"

"Now you are *really* in need-to-know territory." Holly pointed to the map. "This area's woods. There are lakes, campgrounds, plenty of cabins. I'm going to show you a picture of the one we want. It's an interior shot, but it'll give you some idea of what the exterior might look like. But don't eliminate a cabin just because it doesn't seem to fit.

"If you see a cabin, knock on the door, show your credentials, feed them a bullshit story. You know the drill. Tell them anything but the truth.

"The area you're searching is about seventy-five miles northwest of here. Set out from here at four in the morning so you can start searching by daybreak."

Holly reached in her pocket and pulled out a printout of the cell phone picture.

"This is the girl you're looking for."

Quentin started at the sight. "Jesus. What happened to her hand?"

"They cut off her finger."

"Who is she?"

"Her name is Karen Blaine."

"Blaine? Why is the name familiar?"

"She's Congressman Blaine's daughter."

Quentin digested that news. "I'm in."

"You already were."

74

Millie and Quentin rendezvoused at a roadside diner at five-thirty in the morning. They slid into a booth and ordered coffee and English muffins. The only other diners in the restaurant were some boisterous fishermen who were gearing up to head out, and an old man hunched over a piece of blueberry pie. No one seemed to be paying any attention to the young couple.

Quentin fished the map out of his pocket and spread it out on the table.

"I get the east and you get the west," he said.

"That's right," Millie said.

"It's kind of a lopsided map."

"Oh?" Millie said.

Millie hated holding out on Quentin, but it was the nature of the beast. Fudging the map so as not to show Teddy's area had resulted in slight distortions. Some of the cabins that appeared to be hers were actually Teddy's on the real map she had in her pocket.

"It's a big job," Millie said. "But if one of us finishes first, we can team up and help the other."

At the far end of the counter the old man eating pie sighed. He shouldn't have worried. Millie was doing fine.

Teddy had made a good decision to dress as the old agent Frank Grisham. The bald wig was slightly uncomfortable but well worth it. Without the disguise he wouldn't have been able to hang out in the diner. Not at that time of the morning with so few people there.

Millie hadn't recognized him, and she'd been working with him for days. He'd wanted to test out the disguise on her, and be there to personally evaluate the agent to whom he was entrusting a crucial part of the operation. Holly and Millie trusted Quentin Phillips, but a secondhand recommendation was never good enough for Teddy.

It was reassuring to see the young couple. Millie's FBI agent seemed like a nice young man.

Teddy still wasn't going to let him in on what was actually happening.

75

Teddy was having no problem searching the cabins. He was posing as a none-too-swift private investigator and it was very effective. People were pleasant, even kindly, to the affable if somewhat bumbling old man who apologized effusively for the intrusion and frequently referred to his notes as if he were somewhat afraid this was an assignment he was incapable of doing.

"Milton Hasbrook," he said, inventing the name out of whole cloth. "He claims the place is his, and points to a broken window to support his claim."

"A broken window?" the woman who appeared to own the cabin, and probably did, said. "No such thing."

"Well, I'd be very happy to report there was not," Teddy said.

Teddy scratched a lot of cabins off his list, but had nothing to show for it. In between stops he called Millie Martindale to see if she was doing any better.

"How's it going?" he said.

"Well, I'm eliminating a lot of possibilities."

"You skip anything?"

"No. I got in everywhere. Two cabins looked promising. One was a family on a camping trip. The other was vacant. The screen door was open, so I went in. There was no sign of the girl, and no indication she'd ever been there. It didn't look like anyone had been there for a while."

"You marked the location?"

"Absolutely, as a place to recheck. But my gut feeling is no."

"Anybody give you trouble?"

"Not really."

"You have to show your ID?"

"A couple of times."

"What'd you use for a cover story?"

"I told them I was looking for an escaped mental patient with a habit of hiding in people's cabins. They were glad to have me look."

"They didn't ask you why the CIA was tracking an escaped mental patient?"

"I may have had my thumb over that part of the ID. The important part's the official seal and my photo."

"Do you have many more cabins?"

"There appear to be quite a few."

"Have you heard from Quentin?"

"He just called. Nothing yet, but a couple of possibles to recheck."

"We've got to step up the pace. Congress reconvenes at two o'clock to take the vote. We're not going to make it."

"There's four hundred some odd congressmen. Won't a roll call vote take all afternoon?"

"They do it electronically. It won't take more than fifteen minutes."

"I've seen roll call votes where they stand up and say aye."

"That's the Senate. They only do it in the House when the electronic ballot fails."

"How often does that happen?"

"Not often enough," Teddy said. He hung up and called Kevin. "We've got to narrow this down. Have you got anything yet?"

"You'll be the first to know."

Teddy took a breath. "Listen, can you hack into anything?"

"I wouldn't say *anything.*"

"A simple electronic calculator."

"Connected to the Internet?"

"I don't know, and I don't have time to find out."

"What do you need?"

76

Abdul-Hakim parked his car two blocks away, walked down the quiet, suburban street to the unpretentious two-story frame house with the welcome mat and the insufficient security system. The zapper in his pocket raised the door on the one-car garage. This had not been left to chance. It had worked when he tested it the day before.

There was a car in the garage, but that didn't mean anyone was home. The congressman took a car service to work, another detail Abdul-Hakim had taken care to learn. He never left anything to chance, except when Calvin Hancock sprang things on him at the last moment, and then acted like it was his fault when they didn't work out. Abdul-Hakim smiled with satisfaction, knowing he wouldn't have to put up with Hancock much longer.

Abdul-Hakim slipped inside the garage, closed the door, and switched on the light.

The door to the house was unlocked. If it hadn't been he had the tools to pick it, and plenty of time to do so. But there was no need.

A small breezeway led into the kitchen. He set his briefcase on the kitchen table and popped it open. He took out a box of disposable latex gloves, selected a pair and pulled them on. He took a dish towel from the kitchen sink and went back and polished any surface he might have touched on his way in. He'd been careful and there weren't many, still he made a good job of it. It was something that had to be done. He couldn't walk around the neighborhood in latex gloves; he might as well have the word *burglar* tattooed on his forehead.

He left his briefcase on the table and searched the house. It was as unpretentious inside as it was out. The TV in the living room wasn't even high-definition; it was the old-fashioned tube type. He clicked it on and flipped through the channels. It had only the most basic cable. It certainly didn't have C-SPAN. He clicked it off again. The only news reports he'd get in the afternoon would be if something happened. By then he'd be gone.

Abdul-Hakim checked out the rest of the downstairs rooms. There was a small dining room and a study. The study had a wooden desk that had seen use, and a swivel desk chair.

There was a computer on the desk, an ancient affair that still used floppy disks. It couldn't upload data from a computer chip. At least it was attached to a printer, albeit a microdot, not a laser jet.

Abdul-Hakim sighed. He went back to the kitchen, got his briefcase, and brought it into the study. He sat down at the computer and opened the word processing program.

He opened his briefcase on his lap, took out the file folder, and set it on the desk next to the computer. He closed the brief-case and set it on the floor.

Abdul-Hakim flipped the file folder open and began typing.

77

There was no way Kevin was getting close to the Capitol, particularly with a tool kit. He found a loose manhole cover three blocks away. Careful no one was looking, he pried it up and climbed down the ladder below, closing the cover above him.

The sewer was dry, but filled with sludge. He'd ruin his shoes, but aside from at the White House, he seldom wore them. He took his flashlight out of his bag, got his bearings from the GPS in his cell phone, and set out.

A rat scurried down the tunnel in front of him. Kevin flinched, and gave ground. The movement was enough to spook the rat. It stopped, turned, and vanished in the darkness. Kevin took a breath to calm himself and followed the rat down the tunnel.

Even in the sewer he couldn't get close to the Capitol. Padlocked iron gates blocked his progress. No matter. His flashlight beam played across the walls and lit up a veritable maze of pipes and conduits.

Kevin took the printout he'd downloaded from Holly's secure server, and tried to make sense of it all.

Speaker Blaine gaveled the House into session shortly after two o'clock. At least he tried to. He was besieged by fellow congressmen shouting indignant questions and demanding to know how he intended to vote. He banged the gavel again and again with very little effect. He grabbed the microphone.

"Congressmen, please take your seats. It's time to vote on the proposition."

The announcement merely set off a fresh barrage of shouted protests. It took a good half hour for everyone to settle down and get seated. When they were finally in place, the Speaker banged the gavel again, and had the clerk read the proposition. It was the clean, unamended version, to be voted on first.

The reading of the bill was met with shouts of derision. The Speaker was wearing out the gavel.

The Speaker pulled the microphone to him. "All in favor."

"Aye!"

The ayes were met with a chorus of boos.

"Those opposed."

"Nay!"

The ayes and nays were equally loud.

The congressman from North Carolina was on his feet. "Mr. Speaker, I call for a division of the House!"

"There is no need, Congressman," Speaker Blaine said. "It is clearly too close to call. We will proceed with a roll call vote. This is done electronically. When the bill is uploaded on your screen, type in your password and vote aye or nay."

The Speaker set down his gavel, took a sip of water, and mopped his brow. Every congressman in the room had seen his lips move during the voice vote. There was no more fence-straddling. No more equivocation. No more bipartisan bluffing. The Speaker had voted aye. The Speaker had supported the bill. At least some Republican congressmen would surely follow. Within fifteen minutes the bill would have passed.

The Speaker prayed what he was about to do would save his daughter.

The ballot appeared on the screen. All that remained was for him to bang the gavel and tell them to enter their votes.

The Speaker took a breath.

Every light in the room went out.

78

It was actually every light in the Capitol. Kevin couldn't hack into the voting system, at least not in time, and he'd had to rely on the primitive method of severing a power line. It was surprisingly easy to take out the Capitol. The hard part was not taking out the White House, too, which would have wiped out his wiretap.

Considering the notice he'd been given, it wasn't a bad job. The main thing was not getting caught. Kevin hadn't asked what would happen if he did, but he was sure they'd all disavow any knowledge of him.

Kevin hurried back to the manhole. He had a moment of panic when the sewer branched and he couldn't remember which way he'd come. He consulted his GPS. He'd made a wrong turn. He retraced his steps and got back on track. It seemed like forever, but was really no time at all. He reached the manhole and climbed the ladder.

Kevin tentatively pushed up the manhole cover, and dropped it again as several police officers hurried by in the direction of the Capitol.

He also dropped his flashlight. He could hear it clatter at the bottom of the sewer. He climbed down the ladder and fumbled for it in the dark. He found it, switched it on, and climbed back up the ladder.

This time there was no one there. Kevin shoved his bag of equipment onto the street and crawled out after it. He eased the manhole cover back into place and slipped between two parked cars just as an official-looking vehicle hurtled down the block.

Kevin let the bag of equipment hang down his side as inconspicuously as he could, and strolled along with a nonchalance he didn't feel.

The congressmen were not in the dark for long. The emergency lights came on at once, and the backup generator kicked in a minute later. The generator ran the lights and the air-conditioning units and almost everything else electrical in the Capitol building.

There was one glaring exception.

"It doesn't work?" Speaker Blaine said.

335

"No, sir," the young aide said. "It won't run off the generator."

Congressman Blaine felt as if he were losing his mind, as if he were in some bad dream from which he could not wake up. His daughter was going to die unless he managed to complete the roll call vote, and the equipment he needed to take it wasn't functioning. That wouldn't matter as long as the kidnappers knew the vote was going forward, that it would be taken and completed this very afternoon. That was all they had asked for, and all he had promised them. And, by God, he was going to deliver.

"Very well," he said. "The clerk will have to read the roll."

"Sir?"

"We'll do it the old-fashioned way. We'll have a genuine roll call vote. The clerk will read the roll, the congressmen will stand when they hear their name and cast their vote, and the tally will be taken."

"Can that be done?"

"Of course it can be done. What do you think we did before there were computers?"

The young aide, who had never experienced life without computers, had trouble envisioning such a time, but he hurried off to find someone who knew how to conduct a roll call vote.

79

Teddy snatched the cell phone off the passenger seat. "Yes?"

"It's Kevin. I took out the Capitol, but they have a backup generator."

"What?" Teddy said irritably.

"Sorry. I couldn't hack the system so I cut the power lines to the Capitol. Knocked the whole building out. Backup generators kicked in, but they can't run the voting system. They're going to have a roll call voice vote."

"Has it started yet?"

"No, but anytime now. They're setting it up."

"I take it the Speaker hasn't gotten another call?"

"No."

"Okay, hang in there."

Teddy tossed the phone on the seat and heaved a sigh of relief. It had been a gamble, knocking out the voting system. Congress could just as easily have decided to postpone the vote until it was working again. But the Speaker had prevailed. They were taking a roll call vote.

Teddy wondered how much time it bought him.

The aide reported back to the Speaker. "It's all set. The clerk and some of the aides are keeping track of the votes. And they'll be keeping a running tally on C-SPAN."

"Of course," Speaker Blaine said flatly. "They have power for the TV cameras, but not for the voting machine."

When the congressmen had more or less reassembled the Speaker gaveled the session to order. "It is time for the roll call vote. Since the electronic method is not working, the clerk will read the roll. When your name is called, stand and respond 'Aye' or 'Nay' so your vote will be tallied. The clerk will read the motion."

The bill was read again while the congressmen grumbled. No one listened. They all knew what it said, or didn't care and were voting party lines.

The clerk proceeded to call the roll. It went smoothly with no real surprises until he got to the Speaker.

"Congressman Charles Blaine, Republican, Ohio."

The Speaker stood. He looked around the room, paused, and took a breath. "Aye."

Congress burst into an uproar. There were shouts of protest. Congressmen sprang from their chairs. There were cries for the Speaker's resignation.

But when the roll was finally resumed, one thing was immediately clear.

Several Republican congressmen, not wanting to be left behind, were joining the Speaker and voting for the motion.

Speaker Blaine sat in silence, watching his political career go up in smoke.

He prayed it was enough to save his daughter.

80

They'd made a mistake letting her hear her father's voice. It came to her through the fog, cut through the fever and pain, awakened the sense of survival they'd nearly managed to kill. Even now, a day later, in her conscious moments between sleep and delirium, Karen struggled to make her escape.

The big man had done a poorer job than usual tying the ropes. She couldn't use her mangled hand, couldn't use her fingers to work on the knots, but she managed to wriggle her ankles free. Had she picked at the ropes with her toes? Or had one ankle merely slid out?

Karen had no idea. She struggled to her feet and stumbled against the wall, not taking her usual care to make sure the big man didn't hear her. At any moment she expected him to rush in and throw her back down on the mattress and tie her feet.

There was a nail sticking out of the cabin wall. Karen could feel it pressing into her back. She felt for it with her good hand. With her hands tied behind her back, the nail was too high for her to reach, but on tiptoes she could snag the rope around her wrists. She did, and nearly fell over, but the nail itself helped hold her up. She increased the pressure on the nail, trying hard not to squeal from the pain.

The rope wouldn't give. Had she hooked it in the wrong place? Was she actually tightening the knot? Could she risk changing the rope's position on the nail?

The rope gave.

Her hands slipped free.

The pain from the restored circulation was excruciating. She bit her lip hard. Her knees buckled and she slid down the wall, the nail raking her back. She barely noticed. She rolled over, pushed herself to her feet.

The window was open. It was small and high and there was nothing to stand on. It didn't matter. Karen grabbed the sill with both hands, causing fresh spasms of pain, and pulled herself up, climbing the wall with her feet.

It was too much. She slid back to the floor and hung, clinging to the windowsill. Fatigue, delirium, and pain overwhelmed her.

She swayed back and forth with her eyes closed and her head sagging forward on her chest.

She couldn't remember what she was doing.

81

Sam Snyder's car service pulled up in front of his house in Bethesda. It was a car, not a limo, simple and unpretentious. Still, even having a car and driver made Sam uncomfortable. His modest, two-story frame house sat in a development of similar structures. In all his years in Congress he had always been a man of the people, never given any indication of wealth, even though he had plenty. It was important to him, being a close family friend of the President, not to appear to be a member of some privileged class. His wife had thought it silly, always encouraged him to live better, said it couldn't possibly matter. In later years she had wanted him to retire and travel, but his good friend Will Lee had been President then, and he felt he had to stay on. Then his wife had died, and nothing seemed to matter.

Up until her death two years ago, Sam had

always driven to work, a mid-range American car befitting his image. Since her death he hadn't felt safe to drive. He'd space out at stoplights, need to be prompted by the honk of horns. Worse, he'd forget where he was going, set out for the Capitol and wind up at the mall. He'd once made a left-hand turn in heavy traffic, nearly causing a pileup. After that he'd hired the car service, at least for trips to Capitol Hill. But he was always conscious of his neighbors' eyes.

Today there was no one looking, and he wouldn't have noticed if they had been. The veterans aid bill had passed, and by a considerable margin. After the Speaker had voted for it, and after it became clear the bill was going to pass anyway, Republican congressmen had jumped on board just so as not to go on record as having voted against aid to wounded veterans in a generally popular bill that was about to become law.

All in all, it had been a pretty good day. The elderly congressman had a spring in his step as he went up the walk. He unlocked the front door, picked up the mail that had been shoved through the slot, and wandered into the kitchen to allow himself a celebratory drink.

He looked up from leafing through the

mail and stopped dead.

Abdul-Hakim sat at the kitchen table holding a cup of coffee.

"Ah, Congressman," he said. "Come in. Sit down. I've been waiting for you."

Sam Snyder gawked at him. "Who are you?"

"That's not important, at least not to you." Abdul-Hakim set the coffee cup on the table and stood up. He pulled a gun out of his pocket. "Please do me the favor of holding out your hands."

Sam blinked. "What?"

Abdul-Hakim snapped open the briefcase on the table and took out a length of rope. "I'm tying you up. It's for your own good, so it would be wise not to resist."

Sam Snyder didn't resist, but he protested mightily, and kept asking what was going on right up until Abdul-Hakim stuffed a gag in his mouth.

Abdul-Hakim marched him down the hall into the room the congressman had converted into his home office. He sat the old man behind his desk and tied him to his chair.

Sam Snyder struggled against the ropes.

Abdul-Hakim leveled a finger. "You can sit quietly, or I can knock you out. Your choice."

Sam subsided.

Abdul-Hakim satisfied himself that the ropes would hold. Then he went back in the kitchen and retrieved his coffee. It had gotten cold. He was considering making another when his cell phone rang. He clicked it on. "Yes?"

"The bill passed."

"I know. I have one of the congressmen here."

"Ready for Phase Three?"

"Yes."

"Kill the girl."

82

The dull thud and muffled cry woke the big man from his nap. He sat up on the couch and listened for the girl. He heard nothing. He clambered to his feet, stumbled to the back room.

She was gone.

He ran to the window and looked out. He couldn't see her, but he heard branches snapping in the woods.

He turned and ran out the front door.

On the coffee table, next to the deck of cards, his cell phone began to ring.

Karen crashed blindly through the bush. She bumped into a tree, knocked herself down. She struggled to her feet and plunged ahead, taking no more care than before. She had no idea where she was going, she just kept running. She had to get away from something.

The cabin!

She had to get away from the cabin.

The thought jolted her memory, spurred her on.

She tripped over a log, rolled once, and came up running. Her feet were torn and bleeding from running barefoot, but she never noticed, just as she barely noticed the pain when she fell. Which she did again, a nosedive onto rocky ground. She got up slowly, rested a minute.

From off to the right came the sound of snapping branches.

She turned and ran full-tilt through the woods. She barely saw where she was going. She just wanted to get away. The sound of snapping branches was the big man closing in on her, and she couldn't bear the thought. She was never going back.

She tripped and rolled down a hill, and hit the bottom with a thud.

The noises the big man was following faded before going silent. That she'd been able to get this far was unimaginable. She was injured, she was sick, she was delirious. And where could she even go? He hadn't seen another cabin in the area. If he had, he might have broken in to steal some food. All he had was bread that was beginning to collect mold.

If he couldn't find her, she was as good as dead in these woods. He'd be better off just leaving, the hell with getting paid. Except there was nowhere to go, and he had no way to leave. Abdul-Hakim had taken their only vehicle.

There was a crunching noise in the distance. The girl?

The big man's head snapped up.

It wasn't the girl, but a car coming up the driveway. If the girl got to the car and secured help, he'd lose her for good.

The big man turned and began to run.

Karen heard the car engine. It confused her. A car? The only car she associated with the cabin in the woods was the Arab's. If it was his, she should run away. If it wasn't, she should run toward it. A life-or-death choice. How could she possibly tell?

If she stayed out here, though, she would die for sure. She had no idea how far they were from another cabin, or from any form of civilization. It wasn't in her nature to do nothing. She had to make a choice.

Karen climbed to her feet and limped in the direction in which she believed the car to be.

83

Quentin Phillips had a good feeling about the cabin. It had a rough-hewn, semi-finished appearance like the one in the photo, and the big guy on the front porch gave the impression he'd run out to sit there when he heard the car coming. There was something artificial about his casual pose. He seemed self-conscious, like it was an act. Like he was hiding something.

Quentin approached the cabin with caution, his hand surreptitiously touching his gun.

"Excuse me," he said. "Is this your cabin?"

"Yeah," the big man said. He didn't ask Quentin why he was asking, like most people would.

"You had any trouble with prowlers lately?"

"Prowlers?"

"Yeah."

"Nope."

"You been here all morning?"

"Why?"

"If you were gone at all, someone could have gotten in."

"I been here."

"You got plumbing in there?"

"No."

"Then you have to go in the woods."

"What if I do?"

"Someone could have got in while you were taking a piss."

He shook his head. "Only two rooms."

"You checked 'em both?"

The man's face darkened. "Yes, I checked them both."

Quentin flashed his credentials. "Let's check 'em again."

The big man raised his voice. "You want to check out my cabin? You want to see what's in the back room?"

"It's for your own good."

"Like hell."

Quentin thought he heard a rustling noise from inside the cabin, but he might have imagined it. After that he heard nothing.

"All right," the big man said. "Check it out."

Quentin didn't want to turn his back on him to enter the cabin, but the big man clearly wasn't going first. Quentin reached into his jacket and pulled out his gun.

"Hey!" the big man said.

Quentin put up his hand. "The man we're looking for might be dangerous."

Quentin pushed his way into the cabin. It was a very primitive room. He tried to reconcile it with the one he'd seen in the photo, but he couldn't. The girl had dominated everything. Take out the girl and you couldn't tell.

The door to the back room was hung with a cloth. He stepped to one side, raised his gun, pulled the curtain back.

The room was empty, except for a mattress on the floor.

The back window was open. It was large enough for someone to fit through. Quentin stuck his head out, looked around. He wasn't certain, but he thought he saw movement in the trees. A flash of color, like a lumberjack shirt.

Quentin turned to find the big man watching him.

"Nothing here," Quentin said. "You might want to lock that window."

Quentin was on his way out when the man's cell phone rang. The big man answered, said, "Hi, honey," in a totally self-conscious voice.

Quentin got in his car and drove away. A

quarter of a mile down the road he pulled off into the brush, hopped out of his car, and started hightailing it through the woods.

He crept up on the cabin and peeked through the back window.

The first thing he spotted was the lumberjack shirt he'd seen through the trees. It was crumpled up on the floor of the cabin. The man who'd worn it was comforting the big man, who'd also removed his shirt. The two were on the mattress, locked in each other's arms.

They weren't kidnappers, just two guys presumably trying to hide their relationship.

Quentin cursed the time he'd wasted. He hurried back to his car. Hoped it didn't matter.

84

The car was long gone. It hadn't been coming up the driveway. It had passed on the road, driving home from some remote cabin somewhere. It was gone, and with it her last hopes. Karen had run herself out. She couldn't even muster the fear to spur herself on. She plodded along mechanically, one foot in front of the other, walking blindly with no idea why.

The house shocked her back to reality. It was the first one she'd seen, and she'd come a long way. She suddenly realized this was what she had been looking for.

Houses. People. Help.

There was no car out front and no sign of anyone. It was just a cabin, not a house, no one had to live there, but it never occurred to her it might not be occupied. That would be just too cruel.

Karen went up on the porch and knocked. There was no answer, but the door was unlocked. She pushed it open, and called out, "Hello?"

There was no answer. The room was empty.

Karen pushed on into the back room.

The room was empty. The window was open. There was nothing but a mattress on the floor.

There was a rope on the mattress. Another rope hung off a nail on the wall.

Floods of memory washed over Karen. Her knees were suddenly weak. She turned and ran.

The big man stood in the doorway.

The last thing she saw was his fist in her face.

Holly Barker called Teddy Fay. "The bill passed."

"Shit. Call Millie and Quentin. Tell them to speed it up. Don't search every cabin, skip all but the most likely."

Teddy broke the connection and tossed the phone on the seat.

A cabin came up on the right. A gray SUV was parked out front. The tailgate was up. A fishing rod leaned against it. Real, or a useful prop? No time to find out.

Teddy gunned the engine and hurtled down the road.

85

Karen heard the cell phone ring, but it was in a dream. It was a nice dream. The caller was her boyfriend back on campus, and even though she couldn't reach the phone she could hear what he was saying. He was sweet and loving and stroking her hair and wiping the tears off her face as he leaned over the bed where she lay.

It was a confusing dream, what with him being on the phone and there in person, but somehow it made sense, perhaps because it was pleasant, something she wanted, something to be desired.

Also confusing was the fact that her boyfriend was speaking to her over the phone and it was still ringing.

The phone was ringing because the big man was peeing outside the cabin and he had left it on the coffee table. And why shouldn't he have left it there, he was right outside. He never went far, just walked out front and let fly.

Outside, the big man zipped up his pants and went inside just as his phone stopped ringing.

He picked it up and called the number back.

Abdul-Hakim was angry. "Where the hell have you been?"

"Taking a piss."

"For an hour?"

"No, just now."

"Where were you before?"

"Before what?" the big man said. He wasn't about to tell Abdul-Hakim he'd let the girl escape.

"Never mind. It's all done. Wrap it up."

"Wrap it up?"

"Kill the girl."

"Okay."

The big man hung up the phone, fished his backpack off the floor, pawed through it, took out his gun, checked again to see that it was loaded. He heaved himself up off the couch and went into the back room.

The girl stirred in her sleep. He should do it now, before she opened her eyes. He raised the gun.

The shot was deafening in the tiny cabin.

86

The gunshot woke her.

Karen Blaine opened her eyes, blinked uncomprehendingly as the big man pitched forward into the room and fell to the floor. There was a man standing in the doorway, but she couldn't tell who. He looked like a character from a sitcom, some little old man who's crotchety but kindly and knows more than the kids.

Teddy Fay stepped into the room. He knelt by the goon, thrust a gun in his back. The man was clearly dead, but he was still clutching his gun. Teddy wanted to let him keep it. He'd shot the man in the back. It would be important to preserve the scene, to show he'd been about to shoot the girl.

Teddy examined her. Her breath was shallow, her heartbeat weak and thin. He felt her forehead. She was running a high fever. There seemed little chance she'd wake up again anytime soon.

Teddy searched the body. The dead man's wallet was in his hip pocket. Teddy extracted it with a handkerchief, flipped it open. His driver's license identified him as James Grogan. He had a couple of credit cards in that name. The papers in his wallet included a tattered Social Security card, but no other personal documents. The rest were all receipts of some kind.

Teddy replaced the wallet. He searched the other pockets and found nothing of interest.

The backpack in the front room held nothing but a T-shirt, socks, underwear, and a box of bullets.

There was a cell phone on the coffee table, which Teddy slipped into his pocket.

He went out on the porch and called Millie Martindale.

"I just hit the jackpot. Twenty-four Maplewood. Get over here fast. When you get close, call for an ambulance. Don't call Quentin."

Teddy hung up and called Holly Barker. "I've got the girl. The goon who was guarding her is dead."

"You found Karen Blaine?"

"Yeah."

"How is she?"

"She's hurt and sick, but I think she'll make it. He was about to kill her."

"How'd you find her?"

"Just dumb luck. There was a guy peeing in front of a cabin. That fit the profile. We wanted a primitive affair with no plumbing or electricity. I snuck up on the place just in time to see him take a gun and head for the back room. I was nearly too late."

"You shot him?"

"Yeah."

"Did he have identification?"

"He's not our guy. He's white, scruffy-looking."

"That's all wrong."

"This was never what it seemed."

"Any indication who hired him?"

"None. The guy's not going to talk, but I doubt if he knew anything."

"How are you going to handle it?"

"I'm going to let Millie take the credit. I'll have her call you after I brief her. Car's coming. Talk to you later."

Teddy broke the connection just as Millie Martindale drove up. She hopped out of the car and did a double take. She gawked, peered at his face.

"Yeah, yeah, it's me," Teddy said. "Give me your gun."

Millie handed it over.

"Here, take mine." He gave Millie his gun. "Fire a shot."

"Where?"

"Where no one will find the bullet. Into the woods."

Millie aimed away from the cabin, fired a shot.

"Good. Let me have it."

Teddy took the gun back, slid out the magazine, replaced the bullet, and picked up the ejected shell casing from the ground. He wiped the gun clean of fingerprints and gave it back to her.

"Here you are. Handle it some and put it away. Did you call for an ambulance?"

"Yeah."

"Then I gotta get out of here. The girl's on a mattress in the back room. The kidnapper's lying next to her. He was about to shoot her when you stopped him. If you hadn't, she'd be dead."

"I shot him?"

"Yes, you did, and nice work, too. Give me your map."

"Why?"

"Because this cabin's not on it."

Millie handed her map over. "Quentin's got a map."

"Get him to ditch it. Call him now and tell him to make himself scarce."

"What else can I tell him?"

"Anything but the truth. Then call Holly Barker and get your story straight."

Teddy hopped in his car. As he drove off, he could hear the siren of the ambulance in the distance.

87

"It's taken care of," Abdul-Hakim said.

Calvin Hancock exhaled into the phone. "Good. Go ahead with Phase Three."

Abdul-Hakim glanced over at Sam Snyder, still tied to his chair. The little man had quit struggling against the ropes, but he raised his head to glare back. Abdul-Hakim smirked in contempt. A congressman, for goodness' sake. What was the point of rising to power and authority and then living like a pauper?

"Just as soon as I get paid," Abdul-Hakim said.

"You'll get your money when it's done."

Abdul-Hakim was not about to give Sam Snyder the satisfaction of arguing in front of him. He wandered back toward the kitchen as he talked on the phone.

"When it's done, I am out the door. What if there's a glitch? You expect me to leave and trust it will be worked out? Or do you expect me to hang around and get caught?"

"There will be no glitch."

"I'm glad to hear it. Then pay me now."

"We had an agreement."

"We still do. I have my laptop. I can check my bank balance. As soon as it registers a five-million-dollar deposit, I'll proceed."

"You're not dictating terms."

"No, I'm just making sure I get paid." Abdul-Hakim poured himself another cup of coffee, now cold in the pot. "I am not a religious zealot. I am a businessman. That's why you hired me. I can be bought, but only if I am paid. So, the stage is set, the actors are in place, we're ready for Act Three. As soon as you pay your admission, the curtain will go up."

"I don't take orders from you."

"Of course not. You're in charge. I'm an employee, just waiting to be paid."

"Now see here —"

"Call me when you're ready," Abdul-Hakim said, and hung up.

88

Teddy was halfway back to D.C. when the phone rang.

It was Holly Barker. "So far, so good. The cops bought Millie's story, such as it is. She's being released into federal custody just as soon as I can get an agent out there."

"You got one. Quentin."

"I hate to use him."

"It's all right, the cops don't know he's involved. They want her in federal custody, he's FBI. Call him and tell him to get his girlfriend out."

"He's going to want to know what happened."

"And he doesn't get to. We made that clear from the word go."

"He's going to give Millie a hard time."

"Not that girl," Teddy said. "She'll tie him in knots. Did you tell her what to do?"

"Just before the cops came."

"What about the identity of the kidnap

victim?"

"The cops are withholding the name of the girl, largely because they don't know who she is. Sooner or later someone will get the bright idea to run her fingerprints and her rap sheet will pop out. But it's not like she's in the police station. She's in the hospital in intensive care, and the nurses aren't going to take kindly if someone comes at her with an ink pad."

"So, we got time to plan a cover-up."

"Now there's a word you like to hear in Washington."

Teddy had just got off the phone when it rang again. He figured it was Holly calling back with something she forgot, but it was Kevin.

"There's no one in the office," Kevin said, "and I got something you should know."

"What's that?"

"The cell phone that made the call from the cabin — the one where the girl screamed? That phone made another call."

"To the Speaker?"

"No, to a number in Bethesda."

"Did you trace it?"

"Yeah. It's a private house. You want the address?"

"I sure do."

89

Abdul-Hakim was making a new pot of coffee when the phone rang.

"The money's in. Do it."

"I'll just confirm that."

Abdul-Hakim's laptop was open on the kitchen counter. He called up his offshore account and checked the balance. It showed a five-million-dollar deposit. He smiled, picked up his cell phone, which he had set down on the counter. "Yes. The money is in. Consider it done."

Abdul-Hakim closed the laptop and stuck it in his briefcase. He finished his coffee, rinsed the cup, and put it in the drain board. He grabbed his briefcase and went into the study.

Sam Snyder looked up from his desk. When he saw Abdul-Hakim he struggled against his bonds.

Abdul-Hakim ignored him and set the briefcase on the desk. He popped it open, reached in, and took out a gun.

Sam Snyder struggled furiously, and tried to climb out of his chair. Abdul-Hakim untied the bonds, freeing his right arm. Sam Snyder flailed violently, tried to punch him. Abdul-Hakim slapped him in the face, hard. He pinned the old man's arm down, pried his fingers open, and forced the gun into his hand. He twisted the congressman's arm up to his head and pulled the trigger.

Sam Snyder stiffened, shivered, and pitched forward onto the desk. The gun clattered to the floor. Abdul-Hakim hadn't been able to make him hold it very well. Still, enough gunpowder residue would have gotten on his hand. Abdul-Hakim picked it up from the floor, stuck it in the congressman's hand, wrapped his fingers around it, and arranged it on the desk near his head.

Abdul-Hakim took a sheet of paper out of his briefcase. He lifted Sam Snyder's head and slid the paper onto the desk beneath it. He stepped back from the desk to survey the scene.

Teddy Fay stuck a gun in his back.

"Hands up. Don't turn around."

Abdul-Hakim raised his hands. There was something ironic in the gesture, as if he were just toying with the man who held the gun.

Teddy patted him down for a weapon.

Found none. "That's the problem with putting a gun in someone's hand. Then you don't have one." He took a step back. "You can turn around now."

Abdul-Hakim turned, saw Teddy. He laughed, shook his head. "Old man, you are out of your league. You don't know what you're dealing with."

"Maybe not, but I have the gun. Is that Sam Snyder?"

"You don't know?"

"The phone's listed in his name. You sort of messed up his face. What did you put on his desk?"

Abdul-Hakim said nothing.

"Never mind, I'll see for myself. Keep your hands up." Teddy slipped the paper out from under Sam Snyder's head. "Suicide note, am I right? You put a gun in his hand, nothing else makes sense."

Teddy held up the paper, read, " 'I can't live with what I have done.' " He nodded approvingly. "Good start. Didn't bury the lead."

Abdul-Hakim edged closer.

Teddy waggled the gun. "No, no. Are you planning to make a move? I guess I should call for backup."

Teddy set the paper on the desk, whipped out his cell phone, speed-dialed Holly Barker, and gave her the address.

"Get over here. Come alone."

"Why?"

"You just shot a terrorist."

Teddy hung up the phone.

Abdul-Hakim looked amused. "Is that supposed to scare me?"

"I'd be happy if it made you civil. You're not going to be able to overpower me, so save us both the trouble."

Teddy picked up the suicide letter.

I am responsible for the terrorist plot. I hired men to kidnap the Speaker's daughter and force him to manipulate Congress. I hired men to assassinate the hard-line conservatives who stood in his way.

I'm not sorry about Congressman Drexel and Congressman Foster. They were hateful men, they deserved to die. But I'm sorry about the girl. That should not have happened.

I had to end the logjam in Congress and help my good friend Kate Lee. I thought I could make it look like a terrorist plot. But I can't go through with it.

I'm sorry.
Sam Snyder

Teddy looked up from the letter. "Not bad."

Abdul-Hakim stared at him. "Who are you?"

"The real question is, who are *you*? You're not a terrorist, because this never was a terrorist plot. I couldn't figure out what all the connections were, but you just made it easy for me with your phony suicide note. You're the window dressing to make a homegrown conspiracy look like terrorism. I'm willing to bet you're not even a religious fanatic. You're probably just in it for the money. I imagine you expect to make quite a bit."

Abdul-Hakim's eyes flicked to his briefcase.

Teddy shook his head. "You're not very good at this, are you? What have you got in your briefcase? Ah, you brought your laptop. Why'd you bring that? It's on, let's find out."

Teddy opened the laptop, clicked it out of sleep mode. "You didn't close the program. Careless of you. It's a bank account. And what do we have here? A five-million-dollar deposit. Within the last half hour. Care to comment on that? I didn't think so."

Teddy stuck the laptop back in the briefcase. "You're being paid to implicate the Democratic Party in a trumped-up terrorist plot. So, I'm looking for a right-wing extremist with unlimited money. Does that sound like anyone you know? Calvin Hancock, for instance?"

Abdul-Hakim lunged for the gun.

Teddy stepped aside, chopped down on the man's arm with his left hand. His hand holding the gun never wavered.

Abdul-Hakim howled in pain and grabbed his arm.

"Relax," Teddy said. "It isn't broken. It would be if I wanted, but it isn't. You can still raise it over your head. Which I suggest you do right now."

Abdul-Hakim raised his hands.

"Good. Now move over there. Right in front of the desk."

Abdul-Hakim edged sideways. His eyes never left Teddy's.

"Good," Teddy said. "You can put your hands down now."

Abdul-Hakim did.

Teddy shot him in the chest.

Teddy searched the body. The man he'd killed had a driver's license in the name of Abdul-Hakim. Teddy figured it was a toss-up whether or not it was his real name. It didn't really matter now. He had no credit cards in that name, or any other. He must have paid for everything in cash.

Teddy found the CIA credentials in the name of Martin Stark. He slipped them into his jacket pocket. No one knew about them but Margo Sappington, and she was dead. There was no reason to confuse the issue, and they might make trouble for his friend Saul.

Teddy found a set of car keys. He took them out front and pressed the zapper. Headlights flashed on a car in the middle of the next block. Teddy searched the car and found an attaché case in the trunk. He popped it open. The case housed a sniper's rifle, which looked like it had recently been fired. One shell was missing from the magazine.

Teddy had just gotten back to the house when Holly came driving up.

"All right, where's this terrorist I shot?"

"In the study. He's dead. But you were too late to save the congressman."

"What congressman?"

"Sam Snyder. You didn't run the address?"

"You said to hurry."

"I meant it. Come on."

Teddy led Holly into the study. Sam Snyder lay sprawled on the desk. Abdul-Hakim lay on the floor in front of it.

Holly took in the scene. She gestured to the congressman. "He's holding a gun."

"Yeah. He killed himself in a fit of remorse. It's all in his suicide note. I'm taking it with me. You can read it before I burn it."

"Burn it?"

"I'm also taking the ropes used to tie him up. As well as the terrorist's laptop and cell phone. Kevin will have fun with them."

"But —"

"Let's get this done. You be him, I'll be you." Teddy took the gun out of Sam Snyder's hand, gave it to Holly. "Take the gun. Stand in front of the desk. Shoot and miss me."

"Are you serious?"

"Well, I don't want you to hit me."

"Teddy —"

"You need to have fired a gun. That gun needs to have been fired twice."

Holly raised the gun and fired.

Teddy looked back at the bullet hole in the wall. "It could have been a little closer, but it will do."

Teddy took the gun back from Holly. "Now, I'm taking this much-traveled gun, and I'm wiping the congressman's fingerprints, your fingerprints, and my fingerprints off it, and I'm putting it in the dead terrorist's hand. He won't leave fingerprints because he's wearing gloves, but you can't have everything.

"I am taking my gun, which used to be Millie's, by the way, wiping it off and giving it to you. This is the gun you used to shoot Abdul-Hakim."

"That's his name?"

"According to his driver's license. Which may be bogus, since his ID photo didn't show up in any known database. He's not a terrorist, by the way. He was in it for the money. This was an extremist plot to bring down the President by making it look like she was complicit in a scheme to circumvent Congress and implement her own agenda."

Holly's mouth fell open. "How in the world are we going to prove that?"

"We're not going to try. We're going to say this was a terrorist plot, plain and simple." Teddy pointed to Abdul-Hakim. "This is the terrorist. You tracked him here and killed him."

"How did I do that?" Holly said. "For that matter, how did *you*?"

"I got lucky. He called the thug guarding the girl from Sam Snyder's phone. He wanted there to be a record of that call, to suggest that Sam Snyder was contacting his flunky and found out the girl was dead, which drove him to suicide.

"Only the thug didn't answer at first, so he *called back* from the phone Kevin had been tracking. Kevin traced that call and gave me Sam Snyder's address."

"That's what *really* happened. What do I *say* happened?"

"Don't worry about it. I called Stone Barrington. He's going to act as your attorney. He'll make a statement for you."

"No one will buy it."

"Sure they will," Teddy said. "You don't, because you know better. But no one else does. It will sound fine to them.

"Without the suicide note, the information suggests a terrorist attack on Congress, Democrats and Republicans alike. The terrorists' goal was to create havoc and disrupt our way of government."

Holly bit her lip. "I suppose."

"Relax. You got evidence. The guy's car is parked down the street with a sniper's rifle in the trunk."

"He's the sniper?"

"I doubt it. The sniper's most likely the guy in the surveillance video, but that's not our problem. Let the agencies sort it out."

"I'll do my best."

"That's the spirit. And remember, it's all right to be a little bit shaken. You just killed a man who nearly killed *you*. You should probably be checked out by a doctor. By the time you're done, Stone Barrington will be on the case."

Teddy smiled. "Just do as he says and you'll be fine."

90

Teddy and Stone came out of the White House. The sun was shining. The air was crisp and clear.

Holly's hearing had gone well. Stone Barrington stipulated that she shot and killed the terrorist Abdul-Hakim, whom she surprised in the act of killing Congressman Sam Snyder, but would decline to answer any further questions in the interest of national security. A finding of self-defense was a foregone conclusion.

"So, what did you tell the President?" Teddy said.

"What do you mean?"

"Don't play dumb. You couldn't hold out on Kate now. You told her about me, didn't you?"

"Yes. But she won't tell Holly she knows."

"Plausible deniability?"

Stone waggled his hand. "Just barely."

"I assume Will knows, too?"

"I had to take the hit for Kate and tell him that I was responsible for her holding out on him."

"Chivalrous to a fault. So they know I was involved."

"Hey, it will come in handy in case you need another presidential pardon."

"Bite your tongue."

"Now that it's over, you want me to call Mike Freeman and tell him to pull his men?"

Teddy considered. "Leave them in place for the time being. I'll feel better while I'm on the East Coast. Some people are sore losers."

"When are you going back?"

"I have a few loose ends to tie up. I'll call you. Will you be here or in New York?"

"I'll be here tonight. Holly and I never did get a chance to catch up. I'm taking her to dinner."

"Why am I not surprised?" Teddy smiled. "Well, Stone, I guess this is it. Don't take it personally, but I hope I don't see you again."

"Me too. Unless it's on a movie set."

"Billy Barnett you can meet anytime. It's the other guy you should stay away from."

"That should be easy. From what I've heard, he doesn't exist."

And Stone Barrington shook hands with the man who wasn't there.

91

The hit man walked in and sat in the chair facing the desk.

Calvin Hancock sized him up. The man wore glasses, but the eyes behind them were cold.

"They tell me you're the best."

"I am." He said it simply, not bragging, just stating a fact.

"Your fee is exorbitant."

"I'm worth it."

"A half a million dollars?"

"At least."

"I'm told I just have to give you a name."

"That's right."

"You guarantee results."

"I do."

"And yet you expect payment in advance."

"I know *I'll* keep my word. I don't know that about you."

"I pay my debts."

"I'm sure you do. I shouldn't have to

depend on it. And collecting is inconvenient, since I only take cash."

"I don't know your name."

"No one does."

"And yet you have references."

"Did they give my name?"

"No, they just said *him.*"

"That's all anyone ever does. So how did you ask for me?"

"I said I wanted the best. They said you want *him.*"

"You do." The hit man appeared bored. "Just give me the money and give me a name."

"And if you can't do it, you'll return the money?"

"If I can't do it, I'll be dead. I don't plan on being dead. I understand I'm not the first person you've tried."

"Who told you that?"

"No one pays a half a million dollars unless they have to. I'm not the first."

"No, you're not."

"I'd like to talk to the ones who failed."

"You can't. They're dead."

"Did he kill them, or did you?"

Calvin Hancock smiled. "I think I like you. All right, half a million dollars." He picked up an attaché case from the floor and set it on the desk. He opened the top and turned it around. "Hundred-dollar bills. A hundred packs of fifty. Half a million cash."

The hit man stood, picked up a packet, riffled through it. "That will be fine. What's the name?"

"Billy Barnett."

"Who's Billy Barnett?"

"A Hollywood producer."

The hit man frowned. "I don't understand."

"What is there to understand? I give you the money, I give you the name. That's what you said."

"Why is this so hard?"

"If I knew that, I wouldn't be paying you half a million dollars."

"Where is this producer now?"

"He was here in D.C., but he checked out of his hotel and is yet to check in anywhere else. He may have gone back to L.A." Calvin cocked his head. "Will that be a problem?"

The hit man smiled and extended his hand. With his other hand, he fished the hypodermic of untraceable central nervous system paralytic from his jacket pocket.

"Not at all," Teddy Fay said.

AUTHOR'S NOTE

I am happy to hear from readers, but you should know that if you write to me in care of my publisher, three to six months will pass before I receive your letter, and when it finally arrives it will be one among many, and I will not be able to reply.

However, if you have access to the Internet, you may visit my website at www .stuartwoods.com, where there is a button for sending me e-mail. So far, I have been able to reply to all my e-mail, and I will continue to try to do so.

If you send me an e-mail and do not receive a reply, it is probably because you are among an alarming number of people who have entered their e-mail address incorrectly in their mail software. I have many of my replies returned as undeliverable.

Remember: e-mail, reply; snail mail, no reply.

When you e-mail, please do not send attachments, as I never open these. They can take twenty minutes to download, and they often contain viruses.

Please do not place me on your mailing lists for funny stories, prayers, political causes, charitable fund-raising, petitions, or sentimental claptrap. I get enough of that from people I already know. Generally speaking, when I get e-mail addressed to a large number of people, I immediately delete it without reading it.

Please do not send me your ideas for a book, as I have a policy of writing only what I myself invent. If you send me story ideas, I will immediately delete them without reading them. If you have a good idea for a book, write it yourself, but I will not be able to advise you on how to get it published. Buy a copy of *Writer's Market* at any bookstore; that will tell you how.

Anyone with a request concerning events or appearances may e-mail it to me or send it to: Publicity Department, Penguin Random House LLC, 375 Hudson Street, New York, NY 10014.

Those ambitious folk who wish to buy film, dramatic, or television rights to my books should contact Matthew Snyder, Creative Artists Agency, 9830 Wilshire Boulevard, Beverly Hills, CA 98212-1825.

Those who wish to make offers for rights of a literary nature should contact Anne Sibbald, Janklow & Nesbit, 445 Park Avenue, New York, NY 10022. (Note: This is not an invitation for you to send her your manuscript or to solicit her to be your agent.)

If you want to know if I will be signing books in your city, please visit my website, www.stuartwoods.com, where the tour schedule will be published a month or so in advance. If you wish me to do a book signing in your locality, ask your favorite bookseller to contact his Penguin representative or the Penguin publicity department with the request.

If you find typographical or editorial errors in my book and feel an irresistible urge to tell someone, please write to Sara Minnich at Penguin. Do not e-mail your discoveries to me, as I will already have learned about them from others.

A list of my published works appears on my website. All the novels are still in print in paperback and can be found at or ordered from any bookstore. If you wish to obtain hardcover copies of earlier novels or of the two nonfiction books, a good used-book store or one of the online bookstores can help you find them. Otherwise, you will have to go to a great many garage sales.

ABOUT THE AUTHORS

Stuart Woods is the author of more than sixty novels, including the *New York Times*-bestselling Stone Barrington and Holly Barker series. He is a native of Georgia and began his writing career in the advertising industry. *Chiefs*, his debut in 1981, won the Edgar Award. An avid sailor and pilot, Woods lives in New York City, Florida, and Maine.

Nominated for the prestigious Edgar, Shamus, and Lefty awards, **Parnell Hall** is the author of the Puzzle Lady, Stanley Hastings, and Steve Winslow series. He is a former president of the Private Eye Writers of America and a member of Sisters in Crime. He lives in New York City.